"I'm here in Farrington. That's what I called to talk to you about."

"You're in town?" Kayla's pulse raced at the thought of him so near. While she never regretted her decision to call off their wedding, the truth remained that no one had ever affected her the way Ty had. From his charming smile, striking looks, and stirring kisses—at one time he had been her knight in shining armor. Until she'd found out who he really was: a black knight in disguise.

"I know this is a bit awkward." Ty's voice sounded strained. "But I really need to talk to you. . .in person."

"I don't know." The sound of his voice made her lose all sense of reality. She'd left Boston to start a new life without him, something she'd done quite well for the past twelve months. The last thing she wanted was him stirring up buried emotions that were better left to rest. "I don't think that would be wise."

"Please, Kayla. I promise I won't put any pressure on our getting back together. That's not why I want to see you."

"Really?" She didn't believe him.

"I won't deny I still have feelings for you, but I just want to talk. That's it. I have some things I need to tell you."

Kayla bit her lip, knowing she should hang up the phone. She had no reason to trust him. From the beginning of their relationship she'd been naïve not to see him, with his Italian suits and expensive gifts, as nothing more than a liar and a manipulator. What made today any different? Her mother had always told her people never really changed, and she believed it.

"Please, Kayla. I promise I won't put any pressure on you."

"All right." She squeezed her eyes shut and prayed she wasn't making a mistake. *Just this one time.* Then she would never see him again.

LISA HARRIS and her husband, Scott, along with their three children, live in northern South Africa, where they work as missionaries. When she's not spending time with her family, her ministry, or writing, she enjoys traveling, learning how to cook different ethnic foods, and going on game drives through the Africa bush with her husband and kids. Find more about her latest books at www.lisaharriswrites.com

Books by Lisa Harris

HEARTSONG PRESENTS
HP612—Michaela's Choice
HP680—Rebecca's Heart
HP723—Adam's Bride
HP752—Tara's Gold

Don't miss out on any of our super romances. Write to us at the following address for information on our newest releases and club information.

Heartsong Presents Readers' Service
PO Box 721
Uhrichsville, OH 44683

Or visit www.heartsongpresents.com

A Matter of Trust

Lisa Harris

Heartsong Presents

To DiAnn Mills, for taking me under her wing as a newbie writer.

To my husband who graciously reads every one of my manuscripts and encourages me to persevere in this ministry.

And for Beth and Lena for coming along on this adventure with me.

A note from the Author:
I love to hear from my readers! You may correspond with me by writing:

Lisa Harris
Author Relations
PO Box 721
Uhrichsville, OH 44683

ISBN 978-1-59789-888-1

A MATTER OF TRUST

Scripture taken from the HOLY BIBLE, NEW INTERNATIONAL VERSION®. NIV®. Copyright © 1973, 1978, 1984 by International Bible Society. Used by permission of Zondervan. All rights reserved.

Our mission is to publish and distribute inspirational products offering exceptional value and biblical encouragement to the masses.

PRINTED IN THE U.S.A.

one

Ty Lawrence was running out of time. He drummed his fingers against the top of his polished mahogany desk that sat near the window of his office and tried to calm his staggered breathing.

One more minute, Lord. That's all I need.

The computer whirred as it copied the files onto his flash drive. He might not have evidence to hand over to the police for an actual conviction, but he did have enough confidential files at his apartment to keep a government official busy for weeks if Abbott Financial Services was ever indicted. These last files, thanks to an unanticipated inside tip and his password, were the best corroboration he'd found so far in linking the CEO, Richard Abbott, to fraud.

And thirty years behind bars if Ty had his way.

Forty-five seconds left.

Ty stuck a dirty coffee mug and a half-eaten bag of peanuts from his desk drawer into the cardboard box he'd brought from home. The corner office with windows overlooking the city, the company Jag, and a yearly bonus that could pay off the debt of a small, third-world country hadn't been enough enticement to stay in the game. Not since the morning he'd awakened with a hangover and the front page of the *Boston Times* in his lap with pictures of five executives from Orlando arrested for fraud and conspiracy charges.

It was a sobering thought, requiring little imagination to realize that was where he was headed if he didn't get out before it was too late. The unexpected letter from an old friend offering him a job in Farrington, Massachusetts, had cinched the deal. Never mind the fact that he'd make a third of what he made now, drive his old car, and work from an office smaller than his bedroom closet. He'd have a clean conscience, which was worth more than Richard Abbott could ever give him.

Ty glanced at the computer screen. Twenty seconds. His head throbbed. Once Abbott received the resignation letter with his morning correspondence, security would be sent up to escort Ty off the property.

Voices buzzed in the hallway, growing louder as they neared his office. Five seconds. . .

His office door slammed against the back wall as his boss crossed the threshold. Ty looked up from the potted plant he was setting in the cardboard box.

"Good morning, Mr. Abbott."

"What is this, Lawrence?" Abbott's face reddened as he held up the resignation letter Ty had composed the night before on company letterhead.

An expensive, pinstriped suit hung across the older man's broad shoulders and thick waist, but with his late-night drinking, high cholesterol, and added stress that came with trying to defraud a company out of millions, the man would be lucky to live past sixty-five.

"I'm guessing you found my resignation letter?" Ty worked to keep his voice calm and prayed for wisdom.

"I want an explanation." Abbott slammed his fist against the desk and let the letter sail across the top. "I've spent three years grooming you for a place on our management team, and you have the gall to walk out of here with nothing more than a paragraph of explanation?"

"I'm moving to Farrington." Ty spoke his well-rehearsed

lines out loud. It was all the truth. He had just decided to leave out the part that he preferred not to be involved in the company's alleged illegal activities or the fact he was probably avoiding an inevitable arrest by not sticking around and becoming the chief financial officer. "A friend of mine just offered me a job with Farrington Cranberry Company, and I realized it was time to make a change. I'm not cut out for this anymore."

The veins in Abbott's neck began to bulge. "It was because of your father I gave you this job."

Ty dipped his head. "If he were here right now, I'm sure he'd voice his appreciation for all you've done for me."

"You're telling me you plan to up and leave all of this for some underpaid job in some. . .run-of-the-mill cranberry co-op?"

"Granted, the money's not as good, but the stress will be minimal, and I'll have a friend's boat to use on the weekends."

"You've got accounts to deal with. Clients to placate. You can't leave, Lawrence."

Ty slid a framed picture of the seaside off the wall and set it on the desk beside the box, each move calculated and precise. To Richard Abbott, Ty must appear to be another burnt-out employee needing a slower pace of life before a heart attack took his last ounce of breath.

"I've already gone over everything with Reed." The diploma from Stanford came off the wall next. "The Caldwell account closed last Friday, and that's the main account I've been working on for six months. I skipped the two weeks' notice, figuring once I turned in my resignation you'd throw me out anyway. I'm just making it easier for you."

"Easier? I. . ." Abbott gritted his teeth.

He'd never seen his boss speechless before.

Ty forced a relaxed smile. "I'm tired, sir. Tired of the rat race, the competition, and the sleepless nights. I guess I'm just not cut out for this."

"You ungrateful—"

"No, Mr. Abbott." Ty held up a hand. "Trust me when I say I'm grateful for everything you taught me."

When it came to legal issues and taxes, Abbott knew every nuance of the law. The fact that the man was a criminal didn't obliterate his brilliant mentoring skills.

Abbott spun around on his Italian loafers, knocking over a chair with his hand in the process. "Maurice, search him before he leaves. If you find as much as a thumbtack in his possession that belongs to me, have him arrested."

Maurice appeared from behind his boss, 250 pounds of solid muscle in a coat and tie that were a size too small. Ty never had been sure what the forty-something-year-old did at the company, but at the moment it didn't matter. The bald man's lip twitched as he strode across the carpeted room and began digging through the cardboard box, dumping out the peanuts and spilling dirt from the plant across the desk. Next he turned to face Ty with a grin on his face that made Ty's stomach clench. Even four times a week at the company gym upstairs couldn't prepare him for what this man could do if provoked.

What was I thinking?

"Spread your legs and raise your arms."

Maurice patted down Ty's arms and chest. The flash drive burned a hole in his left sock where he'd stashed it.

It's time for a miracle, Lord.

Maurice frisked his right leg. Ty knew Abbott's threat of arrest was far from empty. On hiring, employees were required to sign all but their lives away. And Abbott knew every trick in the book to cover his backside when it came to hiring and firing whom he pleased.

Maurice started on his left leg. Ty's heart pounded in his chest. What had he been thinking when he planned to take the files out of the building with him?

"Mr. Lawrence?" Penny, his secretary for the past three years, knocked on the door.

Maurice looked up. Ty took advantage of the distraction and quickly moved behind his desk to pick up his box and framed pictures. "What is it, Penny?"

"I was trying to transfer a call through to you, but your phone's not working."

No doubt his password had already been deactivated as well.

"Reed will be taking my calls from now on, Penny. I've just resigned."

"Resigned?"

He wasn't surprised at the confused look she flashed him as he slid past her, but neither was he about to wait until Maurice realized he hadn't finished his job. With all that remained of his life at Abbott Financial Services in his hands, Ty hurried down the stairwell, expecting any moment to hear someone shout out his name. The lobby loomed before him with its tiled floor and expensive artwork hanging on the wall. Another dozen steps and he'd be out the front door.

A vision of silky auburn hair and milk-chocolate brown eyes filled his mind as he slipped through the glass doors of the building into the morning sunlight. He might be leaving behind a six-figure salary, but there was one benefit of moving to Farrington. . .Kayla Marceilo. Kayla was not only his ex-fiancée, but also the only woman he'd ever loved. The only woman he still loved. Losing her had been the most foolish thing he'd let happen, and getting her back was likely going to prove to be more complicated than indicting

Richard Abbott in a court of law. Somehow he would have to win her trust and prove to her that turning his life around hadn't been just another one of his acts.

Ty glanced behind his shoulder. He saw no sign of Maurice or Abbott chasing after him. In twenty-four hours he planned to be sipping iced tea and listening to the hum of farmers mowing the banks of the cranberry bogs. And he had no intention of ever looking back.

❧

Kayla Marceilo threw off her shoes and sank into the taupe-colored couch she'd bought at an estate auction last month. Soft strains of Vivaldi filled her two-bedroom apartment as she closed her eyes, relaxing for the first time all day. Moments like these made her grateful she'd moved away from Boston's bustling suburbs to the quiet of Farrington. She loved the winding roads of the countryside filled with apple orchards, quiet woodlands, and the bright red cranberry bogs. Working in her mother's catering business had given her a fresh start, allowing her to leave behind certain ghosts from the past.

The phone rang beside her. Kayla opened her eyes and sighed, wishing she'd remembered to turn off the ringer. She'd spent the past ten hours on her feet, baking seafood cream puffs and petite crab cakes, along with an assortment of other dishes for Sarah Jamison's full buffet wedding reception. Now she wanted nothing more than to sleep for the next week. The answering machine could pick it up. She closed her eyes again, then remembered the answering machine had stopped working three days ago and she hadn't had time to replace it.

She answered on the fifth ring. "Hello?"

"Kayla. It's. . .Ty."

The sound of his familiar voice sent a ripple of goose bumps across her skin. She sat up straight. "Ty, it's been a long time." *Twelve months to be exact.*

"Yes, it has. How are you?"

"I'm good." *Extremely good with you out of my life.*

"How is the catering business?"

Kayla hesitated. Most people assumed she had moved back to her hometown a year ago to work in her mother's catering company. The truth was she left Boston to forget about the man she loved. Had loved, she corrected herself.

She cleared her throat and tried to corral her runaway heartbeat. "We manage to stay pretty busy."

"I remember what a great cook you were. I sure could go for a big helping of some of your cream carmel."

"Crème Caramel." Kayla corrected his French, laughing for an instant at his horrible accent before stopping herself. She had to be careful. Ty Lawrence had a way of charming his way into the stickiest of situations. "Where are you?"

"I'm here in Farrington. That's what I called to talk to you about."

"You're in town?" Kayla's pulse raced at the thought of him so near. While she never regretted her decision to call off their wedding, the truth remained that no one had ever affected her the way Ty had. From his charming smile, striking looks, and stirring kisses—at one time he had been her knight in shining armor. Until she'd found out who he really was: a black knight in disguise.

"I know this is a bit awkward." Ty's voice sounded strained. "But I really need to talk to you. . .in person."

"I don't know." The sound of his voice made her lose all sense of reality. She'd left Boston to start a new life without him, something she'd done quite well for the past twelve months.

The last thing she wanted was him stirring up buried emotions that were better left to rest. "I don't think that would be wise."

"Please, Kayla. I promise I won't put any pressure on our getting back together. That's not why I want to see you."

"Really?" She didn't believe him.

"I won't deny I still have feelings for you, but I just want to talk. That's it. I have some things I need to tell you."

Kayla bit her lip, knowing she should hang up the phone. She had no reason to trust him. From the beginning of their relationship she'd been naïve not to see him, with his Italian suits and expensive gifts, as nothing more than a liar and a manipulator. What made today any different? Her mother had always told her people never really changed, and she believed it.

"Please, Kayla. I promise I won't put any pressure on you."

"All right." She squeezed her eyes shut and prayed she wasn't making a mistake. *Just this one time.* Then she would never see him again.

"I know it's short notice, but what about tomorrow night?"

Thursday. Kayla mentally checked her calendar. She didn't have to be at tomorrow night's catering event, a surprise fiftieth birthday party for Raymond Bridges. Besides, the sooner she saw him, the sooner she could put him out of her mind. "Tomorrow night will be fine."

"Then how about we eat at the country club?"

She hesitated. Another fancy restaurant. Ty knew enough about Farrington to know the Blue Moon was a well-established restaurant that catered to the wealthy in the area. No, Ty had not changed at all. He would only choose the best. This time, though, she knew the real Ty, and she would be ready.

"Come on," he said. "I know how much you love looking over the city lights at night. The view can't be beat, not to mention the food."

"I'll meet you there at seven."

She hung up the phone, shaking inside. If just the sound of his voice could do that, what would she do sitting across the table from him?

Kayla walked to the front closet, opened the door, and rummaged through a box in the back corner until she found the crystal frame that held their engagement picture. She had no idea why she'd even kept the photo. Perhaps a reminder never to make the same mistake again. She ran a finger across Ty's face and wondered how she could have been so wrong about someone. At least she had found out before the wedding and not after.

She would have to be strong tomorrow night. The last thing she needed was to lose her resolve toward this handsome man who had once swept her off her feet before shattering her heart into a million pieces.

&

Ty set down the phone in his newly rented apartment and took a deep breath. For one usually in control, his legs felt as if they were about to melt into the tan carpet beneath him. He hadn't expected the mere sound of her voice to have that effect on him, but on the other hand no woman had ever affected him like Kayla. From the first day they met there had been something irresistible about her. Her laugh, her sense of humor, those dark dreamy eyes, and especially her wide smile that never failed to take his breath away.

Ty glanced around the living room cluttered with boxes, his favorite brown leather recliner, a matching sofa, and a few framed prints that lay against the stark white wall. For a moment he missed his apartment in Boston overlooking the bay. This apartment boasted a view of the parking lot and an all-night diner.

Walking to the fireplace, he picked up the framed engagement picture that sat alone on the mantel. For the photo session Kayla had insisted he wear jeans, a far cry from his usual office attire. She'd been right. They seemed totally relaxed in the picture.

And in love.

"Ty Lawrence, you look stunning." Kayla had fumbled with the collar of his forest-green shirt before the photographer snapped the picture in the park a block from his Boston office.

He'd grabbed her hands and wrapped them around his waist. A strand of her reddish-brown hair, shimmering in the late afternoon sunlight, tickled his nose. "You're the one who's beautiful. I don't deserve you."

He hadn't then. But now things had changed. He'd changed. Maybe he still didn't deserve her, but there was one thing he did know. Life without Kayla wasn't the way he wanted to spend it. She was the missing piece in his heart.

He put the framed photo back on the mantel, longing for the warmth of her touch and the feel of her hand in his. He'd have to be careful tomorrow night. It would never do for him to come across too strong and scare her off. But the truth remained. He still loved her and wanted to marry her. There would never be anyone else for him. If only he could convince Kayla of that.

🙠

Richard Abbott leaned back in his leather office chair and struggled to loosen his designer tie. How had it come to this? Thirty-five years ago he'd been one of hundreds of ambitious Yale graduates with an empty bank account and a suitcase of dreams. Today he was the CEO of a Fortune 500 company. *The Wall Street Journal*, *Boston Globe,* and even *The New York*

Times had declared him one of America's leading businessmen.

Now he faced the threat of indictment, while questions were being whispered throughout office cubicles. He might have $175 million hidden in offshore accounts, but if something didn't happen quickly his name was about to be trampled across Wall Street as the latest executive to have let the lure of money ruin him. He might deserve prison time, but it wasn't going to happen if he could help it. Ty Lawrence flashed in his mind. If he went down, he wasn't going down by himself.

two

"This was a mistake." Kayla twirled around in front of the full-length mirror and studied the sixth outfit she'd tried on in the past thirty minutes. Normally she loved the semi-formal, black and white dress, but today it looked too. . .too inviting. An impression she certainly couldn't leave. How could she have ever agreed to see him again?

She turned to her best friend, Jenny, who sat cross-legged on Kayla's quilt-covered bed for moral support. "So what do you think?"

Jenny flipped one of her bobbed, dark-brown tresses behind her ear and cocked her head. "About the dress or your date with Ty?"

Kayla shot a pointed look, then frowned. This wasn't a date; it was simply a casual get-together. "Both, I suppose."

"The dress looks beautiful. It's the other part of the equation that's incorrect in my opinion."

Kayla fell back on the bed and blew out a sharp breath of air. "You sound like a mathematician."

"I am a mathematician."

Kayla laughed. "Then you sound like my mother."

Her mother's reaction to Ty's dinner invitation had been received about as well as a case of the measles. This was the one disadvantage of living five minutes from her mother's house in a small town where everyone assumed everyone else's business was their own. In Boston, where Sam Peterson ate lunch Sunday after church or who was visiting the Bakers for the Memorial Day weekend wasn't printed in the *Boston Globe*. No doubt tomorrow's leading story of the *Farrington Chronicle* would be a play-by-play recap of her date with Ty. She could see the headlines now: OLD FLAME STIRS UP TROUBLE FOR EX-FIANCÉE. Or if nothing else, stirs up unwanted emotions that were better left buried and forgotten.

No doubt about it. Ty Lawrence spelled trouble. All seventy-four inches of his muscular frame. . .Kayla groaned. If just the thought of his pale blue eyes and square jawline made her pulse race, how was she going to handle him sitting across from her at an intimate table for two?

"Kayla?"

Kayla jerked her head up and caught her friend's gaze. "Sorry. I was just. . ." Just what? Daydreaming about the one man she'd vowed to forget?

Jenny frowned. "You need to focus, Kayla, or he's going to have you wrapped around his little finger by the end of the evening."

"Never."

Jenny began pacing the beige carpet of Kayla's bedroom, her finger tapping the bottom of her chin. "Think of it this way. You're a top military officer—make that a navy seal—and you're going in to face the enemy. You have something he wants—"

"Something he wants?" Kayla's eyes widened.

Jenny stopped in front of the window and quirked her left eyebrow. "He wants you back, doesn't he?"

"I don't know that. He told me he just wanted to talk—"

"And you believed him?" Jenny shook her head. "Please, honey. Guys don't call up their ex-girlfriends just because they want to gossip like a group of old ladies sitting around a pile of quilting squares. Either he's getting married, or he's got a plan to win you back."

"Married?" She hadn't thought of that scenario.

"Forget the married picture for now. What are you going to do if he makes a move?"

"Don't you think you're taking things a bit too far?" Kayla fiddled with the top button of the dress. Any anxiety that had been swirling in her stomach had just escalated a notch or two due to Jenny's incessant suspicions. Which she had to admit had merit. Dealing with Ty required the precision of a surgeon paired with the intuitive skills of an undercover agent.

Jenny obviously didn't agree with her assessment of taking things too far. "You didn't answer my question."

"It's just dinner. What could happen?"

"This is serious."

Kayla blew out a sharp breath. "So what do I wear?"

"The purple dress. It's pretty while extra conservative. It will make him think about how much he lost without giving him the impression you're ready to restart your relationship with him."

Kayla jumped off the bed and pulled the dress from the pile. "Are you sure?"

Jenny let out a short breath. "What's up with you? I might be the mathematician, but you're normally the decisive one."

Decisive until Ty had somehow managed to step back into her life. He'd always left her emotions fluctuating wider than a barometer in a storm. "I'm just nervous."

"And I suppose I'm not helping." A sympathetic grin flashed across Jenny's face. "Listen—you're right. It's just dinner. All you need to remember is that when you're finished you have to tell him you don't ever want to see him again. Now get moving. You have to leave, or you're going to be late. Put on that purple dress."

Kayla held the dress in front of her and cocked her head. "First, remind me again why I broke things off with the most gorgeous guy I've ever known. Handsome, considerate, funny—"

"A workaholic, a manipulator, and a liar." Jenny jumped off the bed and rested her hands on Kayla's shoulders. "Listen, honey. You did what you knew was right, and nothing has changed since you gave him back your ring."

Kayla quickly put on the other dress, her heart still heavy with the reminder of what might have been between them if things had been different. "Why couldn't he have been a Christian? Why did he have to lie to me about that?"

"It will all be over before you know it." Jenny handed Kayla a lavender beaded necklace from her dresser to go with the outfit. "Let him say whatever it is he has to say; then you can close that chapter of your life forever. One day you'll find someone ten times better than Ty. Trust me."

Kayla slipped on the earrings and sighed. "How come your life is so simple and mine's so complicated?"

Jenny lowered her glance. "My life is simple?"

"You know what I mean." Kayla turned around and caught her gaze. "You met Greg and fell in love, and before you know it he'll be asking you to marry him."

Kayla stood once more in front of the mirror. Jenny had been right. The outfit was perfect. The simple, sleeveless dress almost reached her ankles, but most important it was extremely modest. No need to give him any ideas and make him think she was reconsidering their relationship.

Besides, she didn't believe in happily ever after anymore. Let Romeo have his Juliet, and Anthony, his Cleopatra. She ran a successful catering business with her mom, had great friends, and a wonderful church home. . .there simply wasn't room for Ty in her life again.

Then why did the thought of seeing him make her knees weak and her palms sweat?

❧

Kayla prayed the entire drive through the small town, down the narrow country road toward the club and up its long meandering drive. When she found a parking spot outside that overlooked the town below, she said another prayer for added strength. *Keep this line open, Lord. I'm going to need You tonight.*

Acres of velvety green lawns and towering pines surrounded the renovated nineteenth-century farmhouse that loomed before her. She walked past rows of flowers toward the front porch where violin music drifted outside, lending an aura of romance to the evening.

A subject that should have been the last thing on her mind tonight.

She brushed the back of her head with her fingers and tried to calm the nervous flutter in her stomach. Jenny had helped her put her shoulder length hair up, leaving a few loose wisps around her face to soften the look. Of course it really didn't matter what she looked like. She'd listen to what he had to say, and that would be the end of it.

Kayla started up the wide steps, then turned around slowly when she heard a familiar voice call her name. Dressed in khaki slacks and a matching button-down shirt, Ty walked toward her. She drew in a sharp breath.

"If I couldn't drive you here, the least I can do is escort you up to the restaurant, Kayla." He said her name like a familiar caress. Her stomach clenched. "You look beautiful. I always loved that dress. You wore it when you met my mom and dad for the first time."

"I. . .thank you." Kayla looked down at the dress. How

could she have forgotten something important like that? She should have worn her new navy pantsuit. It had no history of the two of them together.

"You're not wearing a tie." In the past Ty had rarely shed his coat and tie because there were few times when he hadn't been working.

"I told you a few things had changed." He stuck his hands in his pockets—a nervous habit she remembered from their two years together. Apparently this evening was going to be as nerve-wracking on him as it was on her.

"Shall we go inside?"

Kayla nodded, taking a second peek at his profile. He looked stunning. Dark hair framed a perfectly proportioned face; from the cleft in his chin to the small scar above his left brow to his blue eyes. They were all so. . .familiar. For a slight second, when he caught her glance, she wanted him to take her in his arms and kiss her.

But that was something she could never do.

"Are you all right?" Ty touched her elbow for a brief second, sending a tremor up her arm.

"Yes." She stammered, disturbed by the lack of control she had over her emotions. "I'm fine."

Ty stopped at the top of the stairs. "Not having second thoughts about seeing me, are you?"

Kayla caught the strain in his voice. "Of course not."

She breathed in deeply and caught a whiff of his cologne. The same cologne she bought him for his thirtieth birthday. Once she had told him it made him irresistible. But not anymore.

Inside the formal entry Kayla glanced toward the Blue Moon's candlelit tables and guests in their starched attire. Ty had always taken her to the finest restaurants, a detail she'd never felt entirely comfortable with. Her family had always preferred a trip to the beach and a plate of soft-shelled crabs.

"Wait." Ty reached for her arm but pulled back before touching her. "I thought we might try the smaller, more informal dining area."

Kayla looked at him with wide eyes.

"You don't mind, do you?" Ty said quickly. "From what I hear the view is just as stunning, and I thought you might like the casual atmosphere better."

"That's fine," Kayla managed to get out. The Ty she knew would have taken her to the finer restaurant to impress her. On the other hand, he had always been good at portraying the image he wanted, and maybe this was just an act. She couldn't—wouldn't—let herself forget who he really was.

⁓

Ty guided Kayla toward the smaller restaurant, afraid that her nearness was enough to make him lose his resolve to keep his distance. From the moment he first saw her, it had taken every ounce of determination he could muster to stop himself from pulling her into his arms and kissing her.

After a year he hadn't forgotten the subtle beauty of her face. But that was not why he had asked to see her tonight. He worked to control his emotions. He could only pray she would accept the one request he had for her tonight. They followed the hostess to an empty table next to the glass walls that overlooked the countryside and in the distance, the town of Farrington.

"Well, here we are." Ty sat down across from her and pulled his chair toward the table, before clearing his throat. "I hope you don't mind hamburgers and fries."

"Not at all. You were right. The view is fabulous." Kayla bit the edge of her lip. He hated seeing her so uncomfortable, especially knowing he was the reason behind her uneasiness tonight.

"I want to hear all about your business." He'd decided to start off by keeping the conversation light and impersonal. "And whatever else is going on in your life."

He caught her glance, and she quickly held up the menu to study it, while tapping her fingers on the table. The waiter interrupted, giving them a moment of reprieve, and took their orders of hamburger and fries.

"Business is good," Kayla said after they were alone again. "We do some birthdays, retirement parties, weddings, and anniversary dinners, but our main thrust is business dinners for local clients."

"Sounds like you've done well." He wasn't surprised at all. Kayla had always excelled in whatever she did, but as a culinary expert she was one of the best. He'd enjoyed more than one home-cooked meal by her while they were together, most of the time while she experimented with different recipes.

Desserts were her specialty. Cheesecake, tortes, sponge cakes, and pies—it was amazing he'd managed to stay in shape while dating her. She'd always had something new for him to try.

"Mom's the one who has really built up the business." She pushed a loose strand of ginger-colored hair behind her ear.

"What's your role?"

Kayla laughed, and his heart melted at her smile. "You name it—I do it. I'm in charge of planning the menus with the clients, but I also do a lot of the cooking and serving."

"Do you miss teaching?" Ty took a sip of his iced tea, keeping his eyes focused on her.

"Part of me does. I know I made a difference in the lives of the students, but I love what I'm doing now so I can't complain."

"You'd be good at whatever you set your mind to."

Her fingers tapped against the edge of the table. "What about your parents? How are they doing?"

He noted how she avoided his gaze and how she'd changed the subject away from her. "They're fine. Still living in Florida and enjoying every minute of being retired. The only drawback for me is that I rarely get to see them."

After ten more minutes of awkward small talk, the waiter placed two hot plates of food in front of them.

"Shall we pray?" he asked.

Kayla glanced at him, a sadness filling her eyes, and a wave of guilt washed over him. While they were dating he had always prayed before they ate. Then she found out the truth that his prayers were nothing more than empty rituals to win her over. How could he convince her that now he prayed to Someone he knew and had an intimate relationship with?

They bowed their heads, and Ty began his prayer. "Lord, I want to thank You for this time Kayla and I have to spend together. I pray that Your name will be glorified in everything we do and say to one another. Thank You also for the food that is set before us. We know that many people around our world don't have enough to eat. Help us to be grateful for all You have given us. In Jesus' name, amen."

Kayla took a bite of her burger as he fiddled with a fry and tried to eat. Conversation came in spurts, a far cry from the easy dialogue they used to share. Halfway through he lost his appetite. What he had to tell her tonight wasn't going to be easy. "I guess there's no use putting off what I have to say." Ty put down his fork. "Please let me try to get through this before you respond."

Kayla folded her hands in front of her and waited for him to continue.

"So much has happened in the past year I don't even know where to begin." He clutched his napkin between his fingers. "Maybe someday I will get around to telling you the long version, but for now I'll just tell you what's important.

"Eleven months ago Jack committed suicide."

"Oh, Ty. I'm sorry." She leaned forward, her eyes wide with dismay. "I didn't know. I'd heard there had been an accident—but suicide?"

"You had just broken off our engagement, and I have to tell you it was the lowest point I've ever been at in my life."

He watched her expression soften at the declaration. Friends since the fifth grade, Jack was supposed to have been the best man at their wedding. His death had been the second life-changing event in his life. One, like Kayla, he'd probably never get over.

"I really am sorry, Ty."

He combed his fingers through his hair. "I started thinking and searching for answers. Things you told me kept going through my head. I never listened to you back then when you talked about God and religion. It was just an act to win you over."

"You did it very well." The bitterness was evident in her voice.

"I know." He couldn't change the past, but he could at least try to make things right now. "I started spending Saturday afternoons with my grandfather. He's the only Christian in my family, and I sat with him for hours trying to prove that this belief you have for a man who died for our sins wasn't true.

"After about two months I quit fighting. I realized I was a sinner. Not only for the way I had treated you, but because I had separated myself from God. From the One who created me."

Ty paused and looked intently into Kayla's eyes. "Six months ago I gave my life to Christ, totally and completely."

The fork she'd been twisting between her fingers clamored against the table. He knew it would take a miracle for her to believe him. He'd played games to get what he wanted and had used religion to win her over. She had no reason to believe him this time.

She tilted her head slightly, and her eyes narrowed. With disbelief? He hoped not. "I. . .that's wonderful."

He held up his hand. "Before you say anything else, I want you to know I understand if you don't believe me. In the past I've lied to you and tricked you. If nothing else, I need to ask you to forgive me. If that is as far as tonight goes, then that's okay."

"But you'd like it to go farther?" Kayla asked cautiously.

He closed his eyes and drank in a deep breath, before looking at her again, dreading the response he knew he deserved. "Kayla, I'm still in love with you, and I think I will be until the day I die. There will never be another woman who understands me the way you do."

Kayla stared out the window across the darkening summer skyline but didn't say anything.

"I also realize you have no reason to believe me, and if I'm ever to have a chance with you then I will have to show you, prove to you, that I'm a different man today from a year ago. I want to win you back, Kayla."

She put her elbows on the table and rubbed her forehead with her fingers. After a moment she leaned her head back and held up her hands, questioning. "I don't know what to say, Ty. You hurt me deeply when I found out the truth. Our entire relationship was based on nothing but lies—your indifferent attitude toward marriage, the excessive social drinking, and, most important, your claims that you were a

Christian. I realized I didn't know you at all."

The truth burned through him, but she was right. He was guilty of every one of her accusations. "You have every right to feel that way."

"You ask me to forgive you?" Kayla took a deep breath and steepled her fingers in front of her. "As a Christian I have to forgive you, but as a human it's going to be hard. To trust you again, well, I honestly don't think I'll ever be able to do that."

He'd expected her to say those words, but hearing them hit harder than he'd imagined. "It's up to you, Kayla. I promise, as hard as it would be if you tell me to walk out of your life, I'll respect your wishes and go. But that's not what I want. If you need time, then I'll wait, as long as it takes."

She shook her head slowly. "I don't know, Ty."

"Take as long as you need, but. . ." He had more news for her and wasn't sure at all how she might respond to his next announcement. "You need to know one more thing. I left my job in Boston and just started working for Farrington Cranberry Company here in town."

"What?" She leaned forward, the surprise obvious in her eyes.

"I might not make the same salary I did in Boston, but it's still a great company to work for. They're expanding rapidly by seeking new partnerships with local farms, like Sanderford Cranberry Farm, for example, just down the road."

"You're telling me you're working at an agricultural co-op instead of your high-paying Fortune 500 job?" Kayla held up her hands. "I don't get it."

Ty drew in a deep breath and reminded himself it was going to take her time to come to terms with his moving to Farrington. That it was going to take time for her to trust him again. "Believe me, I hadn't planned to quit, but some unscrupulous things were going on in Boston, and I felt I needed to get out. I'm still not sure what's going to happen, but coming here seemed like the right thing to do."

"You're going to have to give me a while to think about all of this, Ty. Right now. . .I just don't know."

He caught her gaze and saw the conflict in her eyes. He was certain she still had feelings for him but knew she was trying to hide them. He had changed. If only she could believe him.

three

The next morning Ty dialed Kayla's number from his office phone then quickly hung up. He couldn't do it. Hadn't he promised to give her space? Time to think about what he'd told her? If he really wanted to gain her trust, calling her now would undoubtedly lessen any chances he had of winning her back. Something he couldn't afford to do.

On the other hand, in this situation, not calling her could prove to be just as damaging. He had to call her.

Stalling, he drummed his fingers against his desk and stared out the small window that overlooked Benny's Crab Shack. Too bad life wasn't as simple as choosing between the Wednesday special and the steak and potato dinner. Instead, life was full of complex choices, each with its own consequences. And one thing he'd learned, choosing the right thing didn't automatically guarantee everything would turn out like some happily-ever-after fairytale.

He'd realized that last night. Running his fingers through his hair, he wondered if there really was a chance at all for her ever to trust him again, or if he was simply fooling himself with his wishful thinking. At least last night had gone better than he'd expected. He'd been afraid she'd leave in the middle of his confession, but instead she'd listened to him, forgiven him and, in his mind anyway, hadn't completely dismissed the idea of their getting back together.

He picked up the phone and started dialing. Of course she hadn't encouraged him either, but he could live with that. He was willing to do whatever it took to prove to her he wasn't the same man she'd known a year ago.

She answered on the first ring. "Hello?"

He recognized her sleepy voice and smiled. She always had taken every chance she could to sleep in. Realizing how well he knew her only made him miss her that much more. "I'm sorry. I didn't mean to wake you up."

"I wasn't sleeping. I'm just not fully awake yet." Kayla's voice turned cool and professional. "I didn't expect to hear from you so soon."

"I know." He cleared his throat as his well-rehearsed lines evaporated into the morning breeze. "This. . .this call isn't about us. I promised to give you as long as you needed, and as hard as it might be I aim to keep my promise. The reason I'm calling is that something happened at work, and I was afraid it might prove to be a bit awkward."

"What do you mean?"

He shut his eyes for a moment and pictured her snuggled under the favorite quilt her mother bought her for her twenty-eighth birthday. Losing her for a second time would hurt worse than before, but he had to be honest with her. "The company I'm working for now is looking for someone to cater a number of upcoming events."

"And you recommended me?"

"I didn't have to. Your name came up, and they're giving you a call this morning."

"Wow. That's great." For an instant she seemed to forget who she was talking to, because the guarded tone in her voice disappeared. "My mom's been trying to get new accounts with several of the local businesses."

"I felt like I needed to let you know this wasn't some scheme of mine to see you." If he was going to get her back, he would have to be totally honest with her, no matter what the cost.

"I appreciate your telling me."

"Listen—I've got to get back to work."

"Ty. . ." There was a pause on the line.

"Yes?"

"I know you haven't been here long, and, well, I wondered if you had found somewhere to go to church on Sunday."

He froze at her invitation. "Actually no. A guy I work with invited me to his church, but I haven't made any commitments."

"Why don't you pick me up at nine?" She quickly gave him directions.

"Are you sure?"

"Yes."

"I'll see you Sunday then."

Ty hung up the phone wondering if he'd heard her correctly. Had she actually invited him to pick her up for church? He took a deep breath and tried to slow his racing pulse. He hadn't let himself hope she'd give him a second chance. Hadn't let himself dream of the possibility that he could win her back.

Give me wisdom, Lord. You know how much I love Kayla, and yet I know I have to love her enough to let her go if that's Your will.

All he could do now was pray that was something he wouldn't have to do.

❦

Kayla stood in the large kitchen they used for their catering business in town, chopping fresh mint for a couscous salad and replaying in her mind the conversation she'd had this morning with Ty. She had no idea what had gotten into her. Instead of standing firm in her resolve to stay away from him, she'd just complicated matters. He could have gone to church anywhere; yet she'd rushed blindly ahead without thinking and invited him to go with her. Ty was the man who had broken her heart. Why did she keep forgetting that?

Her mother bustled into the kitchen out of breath, with a box of fresh peaches in her hands. "How long until the salad's ready? I need to finish up the shortcake, then hurry across town to the Lamberts' and make sure their tables will seat thirty for tonight's reception."

"Relax, Mom." Kayla leaned against the counter. "The tables will work fine. I checked it out yesterday."

"You did, didn't you? I'd forgotten." Her mom set the box on the counter and rubbed her temples with her fingers. "I don't know what's wrong with me today."

A glance at the calendar that morning had reminded Kayla to be prepared for her mother's moodiness. She'd been seven when her father had been killed in a car accident, and while she didn't remember much about him her mother had never forgotten the pile of bills he'd left behind, or the fact that they'd found alcohol in his blood and an empty six-pack of beer in the back seat. She'd also never forgiven him for the embarrassment of being the last one to find out that her husband's drinking had spiraled out of control.

Maybe some good news would lift her mom's spirits.

"We have a new client." Kayla checked her mom's expression and was thankful to see the smile that played on her lips.

"Really? Who?" Her mom pushed up her gold-rimmed bifocals and raised her penciled brows in interest.

"Someone from Farrington Cranberry Company called this morning to set up a couple of events." She hesitated. "Ty works for them now."

The moment the words left her mouth, Kayla knew she shouldn't have spoken them. Her cautionary attitude toward Ty was only surpassed by her mother who had never forgiven him for breaking her only daughter's heart.

"What?" Her mom didn't bother to mask the look of surprise on her face and placed her hands on her hips. "What happened to your resolution to close the door on Ty Lawrence for good?"

"It's okay, Mom. Nothing has changed. I'm over Ty, 100 percent, and this is just business. Ty had nothing to do with it." She knew she sounded as if she was trying to convince her mother. Truth was, she was still trying to convince herself.

"And you believed him?" Her mom wrinkled her brow and shook her head. "Kayla, I'm worried. First dinner and now this?"

"You know we can't afford to turn away clients, and besides, we'll be catering for his company, not for him personally." Kayla picked up a ripe tomato and resolutely began chopping. "I probably won't even see him."

Her mother shook her head and started cutting up some peaches. "All that man has ever done is lie to you."

"That's not true, Mom."

"Have you so quickly forgotten?" Her mom tossed a pit into the trashcan. "Kayla, take a look at the situation. Ty knows exactly how to get to you. He heaps on the charm and claims he's something he's not. Now you tell me. How's that any different from the last time?"

"I don't know, Mom." Kayla picked up the pile of mint and tomatoes and dumped them into a fluted glass bowl. "What am I supposed to do? He's put no pressure on me and even promised me that if I tell him to leave he'll walk out of my life forever."

Her mother shook her head, her short auburn curls bouncing with emphasis. "I thought you wanted him out of your life."

"I do."

She couldn't tell her mom she'd invited him to church. Not that her mom would be attending Sunday's worship service. Rosa Marceilo had buried her faith in God the same day she buried her husband. And unless someone decided it was their business to inform her mother of Kayla's moment of weakness, then she didn't even have to know. Besides, it was just a onetime thing. It wasn't as if it would become a habit where he picked her up each week. No. Nothing had really changed. Ty Lawrence was out of her life for good.

Kayla sliced a lemon in half and squeezed the tart juice into the salad. The only problem was, if he was out of her life, then how come she couldn't get him out of her heart?

❧

Kayla woke up Sunday morning with a knot in the pit of her stomach. In a little over an hour Ty would be by to pick her up. She rolled out of bed and made her way to the bathroom to brush her teeth. Her mother had once compared Ty to her father who had at one point claimed to be a Christian. After he died, she began telling story after story of Christians whose actions failed to follow their high and mighty words of love and forgiveness. Jenny's family, though, had shown Kayla another side of Christianity. She'd seen the way they acted out their faith, and because of their example she'd committed her life to Christ when she was fourteen.

Her mother's resentment hadn't stopped Kayla from praying her mother would someday realize Christians were by no means perfect. They were only forgiven. Saved by Christ's blood, thus making them perfect in God's eyes.

Kayla's thoughts switched back to Ty. If Christ had forgiven all of her sins, then surely she could forgive Ty, whether or not he was telling the truth. That was the hard part. She wanted desperately to believe him, and yet how could she?

Lord, I need You to help me find a way to forgive him the way You have forgiven me.

An hour later Kayla picked up her Bible from the bed and walked out of her room, not even bothering to glance at the full-length mirror. It didn't matter what she looked like. Forgiveness didn't mean she had to put her heart on the line a second time. A fact she intended to make perfectly clear to Ty today.

The doorbell rang, and Kayla hurried to answer it, praying she wouldn't drop her guard once she saw him. He stood at her door, Bible in hand, with a smile that would have melted the hearts of most women.

Not mine, she reminded herself.

"You look beautiful this morning," he said, as she locked the door behind her and followed him to the car.

Kayla glanced down at her raspberry skirt and matching blouse. "Thanks."

She could have said the same to him but didn't. Still, he did look gorgeous in a gray suit and sky-blue shirt with matching tie. He always knew how to dress.

Ty hurried around to open the passenger side of his two-door car, allowing Kayla to slide into her seat before he shut the door. Her heart hammered in her chest as she leaned back and tried to relax. The car, like Ty, was so familiar. They had dated in this car, and he'd kissed her here for the first time. Kayla slammed the door on the memory.

"You'll have to tell me how to get there," he said, pulling out of the parking lot.

Kayla proceeded to give him directions to the church she had been attending since moving back home.

"Your boss's secretary called our office Friday morning," Kayla began, wanting to ensure that the conversation stayed away from anything personal. "I appreciate your letting me know about the job."

"No problem. I hoped you'd be pleased."

"I was. We already have several functions scheduled for them. Next Friday we'll be providing an Italian dinner for the board and their spouses."

"I'm sure it'll be a hit."

"Then in two weeks we'll be serving a Southern-style barbecue for the staff."

"That will be no small dinner."

"Eighty-five people," Kayla said, after telling him to turn left at the light.

"I'll be there for that one. What's on the menu?"

"The powers that be wanted something different, so we decided to try some Southern fare. Barbecue, beans, corn on the cob, cornbread, and cherry cobbler for dessert."

"I can't wait."

The best thing to do was not work that night. Jenny, her mom and the extra servers they would hire could handle things without her. "Jenny took a year off from teaching and is working for us part-time."

"She planned to be your maid of honor."

"Yes." Kayla wished he hadn't brought up their wedding. There was too much history between them.

"It'll be good to see her."

She grimaced. Without a doubt she needed to make her decision clear and the sooner the better.

Thirty minutes later Kayla sat next to Ty on the pew, barely hearing the words of the sermon. How many times had they gone to church together as she unknowingly succumbed to his deception of being a believer? It had all been an act. What was she doing here with him again?

" 'You see, at just the right time, when we were still powerless, Christ died for the ungodly.'"

Kayla's ears perked up as Pastor Jenkins read from the fifth chapter of Romans. " 'Very rarely will anyone die for a righteous man, though for a good man someone might possibly dare to die. But God demonstrates his own love for us in this: While we were still sinners, Christ died for us.'"

Kayla looked at Ty. For the past year she had seen him as a sinner. One who took advantage of her and in turn broke her heart. Never once had she found the courage to ask God for Ty to find forgiveness in Jesus Christ, a redemption that came so freely.

Now that Ty said he claimed that forgiveness, she refused to believe him because one thing still haunted her. What if he was still lying?

"Now look back at chapter four and verses seven and eight," the minister continued, and Kayla forced herself to listen. " 'Blessed are they whose transgressions are forgiven, whose sins are covered. Blessed is the man whose sin the Lord will never count against him.'"

Kayla swallowed hard and glanced at Ty's lean form. His gaze rested intently on the minister as if he were soaking in the message. Was it just a coincidence that today's lesson spoke on forgiveness, or was God trying to tell her something?

≈

Ty sat across from Kayla at a corner table in one of the local restaurants. He'd enjoyed the church service, in spite of the fact that he'd been afraid she regretted the moment she'd invited him. If she had, he saw no sign of it in her friendly smile as she introduced him to some of her friends. Afterward she'd told him they needed to talk, and he'd suggested lunch.

"So what did you think about the sermon?" Kayla asked

after the waitress had brought them their lunch.

Ty took a bite of his steak sandwich before answering. "It reminded me of just how amazing it is that Christ died for me and how unworthy I am. And I'm thankful I finally figured out I need Him." Ty paused. "I know this is hard for you, Kayla. If our places were reversed, then I would have a difficult time believing you. I only hope I can show you by the way I act that I'm not the same man you broke it off with a year ago."

She nodded. "I am having a hard time trusting you. I want to believe you. I want to believe you've changed, and yet how can you really expect me to do that?"

Ty put down his sandwich and looked at her intently, shaking his head. "I don't know, Kayla. I realize it won't happen overnight."

She still had the same effect on him. He couldn't think straight around her. He reached across the table and took her hand. Kayla pulled hers back as if he had touched her with a burning coal, and immediately he regretted his actions. "I'm sorry, Kayla. I shouldn't have done that. I just. . ."

"Forget it."

What had he been thinking? Ty forced himself to take another bite. Surely she still felt something for him. To have her so near and yet not be able even to touch her was excruciating. He tried to think of something nonpersonal and nonthreatening to say. He had to take it slow so they could get to know each other again.

"I'm enjoying my new job." Surely work was a safe topic. "The company I'm working for is great."

"Really?" Kayla took a bite of her salad, looking as if she were making herself eat. "What do you do?"

"I'm sort of a financial adviser."

The waitress came to refill their drinks, and Kayla pushed her plate aside. "Sounds like fun." Kayla's tone was dry.

Ty sighed. He'd honestly thought that when she invited him to church it had been an unspoken truce, but apparently he was wrong. He watched Kayla check her watch for the tenth time and wondered what he should do.

"Ty. . ." She paused and reached for her purse. "This just isn't going to work. I never should have agreed to see you in the first place. I'm sorry, but we won't be seeing each other again." Without another word Kayla got up from the table and walked out the door.

Just as she had a year ago.

Ty's heart sank as he watched Kayla leave the restaurant, shocked at her abruptness. She must have been sitting there the entire lunch trying to figure out how to tell him there wasn't a chance for them. He had known it wouldn't be easy to win her back, but somehow he'd convinced himself it would work out.

He knew he had changed, but how could he convince Kayla? He possessed a deeper love for her than he had a year ago. If only she could find it in her heart to give him another chance. Ty paid the bill for the uneaten food and left the restaurant.

❧

Kayla felt nauseous as she walked the six blocks home. Things had not gone the way she had intended. She'd planned to be a bit gentler and explain her reasons, but instead it had all come out at once.

What else could she have done but leave? If she hadn't left the moment she did, she knew she would have given in to him. When he took her hand, her entire body had melted at his touch. She couldn't trust him, and she couldn't see him again. There was simply no other way around it.

four

Kayla glanced across the lofty barn that had been converted into a meeting hall and wished she could slip off her shoes. The front half of the structure was filled with a dozen round tables covered with red-checkered cloths. She'd spent the afternoon making centerpieces from cowboy hats, balloons and bandanas. Most of the employees of Farrington Cranberry Company had already filled their plates with the Southern spread and were enjoying the warm July evening, thanks to the bigwigs who were picking up the tab.

The corporate headquarters had made the decision five years ago to settle in the small valley outside Farrington. Landing a catering contract with the company that sold everything from cranberry juice to dried cranberries to cranberry muffins nationwide was a huge blessing for Marceilo Catering. And tonight was key to future catering jobs. Already Kayla had received several compliments on the food as people migrated back to the buffet line for seconds. Her mother had grown up in Memphis and could make barbeque like a pro. They'd added cranberry chutney and cranberry apple crisp to the menu to impress the VIPs, a decision that hadn't gone unnoticed.

"Looks like you've outdone yourself once again."

Kayla glanced up to see Ty filling his plate with a mound of potato salad. A lump swelled in her chest. "Ty. . .I didn't think you were here tonight."

"I got snagged into a conversation outside and somehow missed the first lineup."

She gnawed on the edge of her lip. Great. Now he was going to think she'd been looking for him. Except she hadn't. Not really. Nothing more than a few lingering gazes across the crowded room as she made sure the servers were doing their job and the food warmers stayed full. Of course, that wasn't to say that in the past two weeks she hadn't thought about picking up the phone and calling him to apologize for her abrupt departure at the restaurant. But every time she started to call she managed to convince herself Ty Lawrence wasn't worth a phone call. The truth was, she didn't owe him anything.

He moved to the beans, and she pretended to stay busy by filling a warming pan with more barbeque beef. Over half the employees had taken the evening's theme seriously and dressed in Western shirts and boots. A number of the men even sported cowboy hats. Ty was no exception. Red plaid shirt, fitted blue jeans, and a black Stetson were enough to woo the heart of any cowgirl. Even she had to admit the rugged look fit him. But Ty always had put appearances first, and she'd learned the hard way that appearances could be very deceiving.

Kayla handed off the empty pan to one of the servers. She was going to have to get rid of any guilt that lingered, because tonight was proof this was a small town and their running into each other was inevitable. If only he didn't manage to tie her emotions into a double knot. At the moment her knees felt like jelly and her heart like the bass drum in a high school marching band. Definitely not a good sign that she'd forgotten the six-foot-two cowboy standing in front of her.

But why does he have to look so amazingly gorgeous?

Ty added a piece of jalapeño cornbread to his plate. "You've got quite a spread here. I don't remember the last time I had barbeque, but it smells absolutely heavenly."

"Once you've got your food, drinks are at the table over there." She cringed at her harsh tone. He'd asked her to forgive him, and she'd practically thrown it back in his face. So much for setting a Christian example. "Love your neighbor as yourself" and "Forgive as the Lord forgave you" were commands she was struggling to follow. Which made it look from the surface as if Ty was more of a Christian than she was. If he really was a Christian at all. Could she help it if her history with the man dictated she guard her heart tighter than the First Bank of Farrington?

"I don't believe I have ever seen you quite so. . ." Kayla searched for the right word.

"So casual?" He chuckled.

"It was always an effort to get you to relax long enough to change out of a tie and jacket and into a pair of blue jeans."

Ty's blue eyes widened. "So you approve?"

"I. . .yes," Kayla stammered.

This definitely wasn't fair. She should have taken her mother's advice and skipped tonight. Except she couldn't keep running. Had she already forgotten she was over him—100 percent? There was no need to run. And the look was perfect for him. All he needed now was a lasso and a mechanical bull.

"Now this looks delicious." He put a spoonful of maple-roasted sweet potatoes on his plate, gave her a slight nod then walked over to the drink table.

Kayla's jaw dropped. He acted more interested in the food than in her. She grabbed the empty pan and headed for the kitchen. Of course, that was exactly the way it should be. She'd told him the relationship was over, and he'd finally accepted it. Wasn't that what she wanted?

As much as she tried not to notice, Kayla spent the next

hour watching Ty mingle with his coworkers. He'd sat down at a table near the buffet giving her the opportunity to observe him—if she wanted to.

Which of course she didn't.

While the servers normally refilled the drinks, she walked by his table with a pitcher of tea and caught the beginning of a dirty joke by a red-headed man wearing an orange bandana around his neck. With his typical charm, Ty managed to smoothly change the course of the conversation. She was impressed. Not that she didn't expect him to be sociable and charming; but as she strategically moved throughout the room and caught pieces of his conversation she was surprised the conversation didn't center on work. A year ago work was the only word in his vocabulary.

But he knows I'm in the room.

Out of the corner of her eye she watched a woman wearing jeans a size too small and a low-cut white blouse approach Ty and stand behind his chair. Ripples of laughter erupted from the beautiful colleague's mouth.

"Miss Marceilo?"

Kayla jumped. "Yes?"

A tall, willowy woman wearing a jeans skirt and a fringed jacket reached out and shook her hand. "I'm one of the vice-presidents, and I wanted to let you know I'm quite impressed with all your catering company has to offer tonight."

A roar of laughter came from Ty's table, but Kayla ignored the urge to turn away.

The executive shot her a knowing smile. "He's quite a ladies' man."

"Excuse me?" This time Kayla followed the other woman's gaze.

"Ty Lawrence. He's one of our newest employees, and he

seems to have won the hearts of the women."

Kayla swallowed hard. So the truth was about to come out. As far as she knew he'd never cheated on her while they were together, but on the other hand she wouldn't have put it past him.

The woman turned back to her. "Funny thing is, rumor has it he isn't interested in any of them."

Kayla cocked her head. "What do you mean?"

"From what I hear there's only one woman in Ty's life."

"There is. . .I mean. . .who?" Kayla worked to steady her breathing. *He had told people he was still in love with her. . . .*

"That I don't know. I was told there was some girl who captured his heart, and he moved here to win her back. Knowing him, he'll get what he wants. Anyway, I just wanted to let you know you'll be hearing from us again for other events."

"Thank you." Kayla swallowed hard. *I'm over him. I'm over him. . . .*

The rest of the evening flew by as she worked with her mother and the staff to ensure the service continued to be exceptional. Once the speaker had finished, they got everything cleaned up and packed in their van.

"I think that's the last of it." Her mom slammed the door shut, then rested her hands against her hips. "I noticed Ty appeared to keep his distance."

Kayla frowned. "I told you he would."

"His word is worth about as much as an outlaw's straight out of the Old West. He's just biding his time. You wait and see."

It certainly wouldn't be the last time her mother reminded her she was unhappy with Ty's move to town, but Kayla refused to be dragged into another argument. Glancing into the front seat of the van, she tried to remember where she left her purse. Nothing. She opened the door again and began rummaging through the boxes they'd stacked.

Her mom stood beside her with the van keys dangling in one hand. "What are you looking for?"

"My purse."

"Didn't you put it in one of those cabinets behind the buffet table?"

Kayla slammed the door shut. "You're right. I'll be back in a sec."

&

Ty grabbed his hat from the table and turned to leave with a few of the guys who had lingered behind visiting. He'd enjoyed the chance to meet some more of his coworkers, but it had been impossible for him not to be aware of Kayla's presence the entire evening. He'd wanted to tell her how beautiful she looked in her smart black skirt and red blouse as she bustled around the room ensuring everyone was taken care of—but he hadn't dared.

One of his coworkers came up beside him and slapped him on the back. "Why don't you join us down at Willy's Bar, Ty? Nothing like getting a little drunk on a Friday night."

Ty's hesitation lasted only a moment. A year ago he would have jumped at the invitation. Tonight, getting drunk with a bunch of buddies held none of the appeal it used to. "You know, guys, I think I'll just head on home."

"What's the matter?" A second guy unbuttoned his collar. "You're not one of those Christians who can't stand to have a little bit of harmless fun, are you?"

Ty shook his head. "Actually, I love to have fun just like the next guy, but drinking and waking up with a hangover the next morning doesn't strike me as entertaining anymore. And yes," he added, smiling, "I am a Christian."

He stood there as the men stalked off without him. He might lose a few friends in the process, but the peace he had from his new commitment was worth it.

"Hey."

Ty spun around and felt his heart take a nosedive. "Kayla? I thought you'd left."

"I did, but I forgot something." She held up her purse and shot him a lopsided grin.

His heart raced as he gazed at the one woman he'd given his heart to.

Her gaze swept the floor. "I've been watching you tonight."

"What do you mean?"

"Never a bad word about anyone. Never a dirty joke thrown in for laughs. Still, you knew I was in the room, and I never could be sure it wasn't just an act."

His stomach clenched as he waited for her to continue.

"It's not an act, is it." She said it as a statement rather than a question.

He fiddled with the brim of the Stetson and tried to keep his hands from shaking. "I told you it wasn't."

"I heard you tell those men you're a Christian, and I'm sure they won't let you down easy. This time you had no idea I was in the room."

"No, I didn't." Ty's voice held steady as he looked at her. He should feel ecstatic that she believed him, but part of him wanted simply to walk out of the room. He refused to spend the rest of his life proving to her who he'd become. "Is this what you were looking for, something to substantiate that I am who I say I am?"

"Yes, no, I. . .I don't know." She took a half dozen steps toward him, then stopped.

The room was empty now, and all he could hear was a hum

coming from the kitchen and his pulse pounding in his ears. "I won't play games, Kayla. You told me things were off, and I gave you my word I would accept your decision."

She slung the strap of her purse over her shoulder. "It's funny, but as hard as I tried to put you out of my mind this past year, your coming has made me realize I'm not over you. Maybe I'll never be over you."

He was sure he hadn't heard her correctly. Or maybe he was only dreaming. Because Kayla was out of his life. Unless. . . "What are you saying?"

Kayla continued to bridge the gap between them until only a few inches remained. "You've changed, and I. . ."

She stopped, close enough for him to catch a drift of her sweet perfume and see the tears that pooled in the corners of her eyes. How many times in the past few months had he prayed God would let Kayla see him for who he had become? That somehow he could erase the doubts that stopped her from trusting him?

He wiped away the tear that slid down her cheek. "What is it, Kayla?"

"It's you. . .and me. I—I don't know what I'm trying to say."

He'd promised himself he would give her the space she wanted, but with her lips hovering just below his face he did what any other man would have done in his situation. He leaned down and kissed her, ignoring the Stetson that dropped to the ground as he wrapped his arms around her waist.

A flood of memories washed over him. The scent of honey and roses engulfed him. It was as if the past year never existed between them. . .except it had. And even he couldn't expect them to simply continue where they left off. There was too much hurt folded into their relationship. Too much mistrust.

Pulling away, he cupped her face in his hands and stared into her eyes. "I've missed you so much, but I never expected this."

Kayla took a deep breath and stepped back, but her hands still rested against his chest. "Ty, I—"

"I'm sorry. I promised I wouldn't push you."

"No. This is just as much my fault." She looked down, and he felt a wave of regret wash over him.

He tried to read the expression in her eyes, but her dark lashes swept against her cheeks as she stared at the floor. Surely she didn't regret their kiss. To lose her again—like this—was more than he could handle. He might as well move back to Boston and let Mr. Abbott feed him to the lions.

He tried to swallow the lump that swelled in his throat. "So what happens next?"

"I don't know."

"If you regret—"

"No. I don't regret anything. This has just completely taken me by surprise." She looked up at him, and her lips curled into a smile. "We've both changed in the past year. I need to get to know you again."

"Fair enough." He leaned forward and brushed his lips against her forehead, still not believing she wasn't kicking him out the door.

"Ty." She looked up at him and laughed. "I'm serious."

"So am I." He kissed her one more time before pulling away. "I told you I'd always love you. I just never imagined there was actually hope for the two of us."

❧

Kayla felt her head spin, still uncertain of what had taken place in the past five minutes. His eyes were brighter than she remembered. Blue like the Atlantic Ocean on a warm summer's day. And they seemed to reach all the way into her soul. One thing was clear. Ty had kissed her—and she'd been all too willing to kiss him back. She looked up at his jawline that was sprinkled with a touch of stubble making him look even more like the rugged, handsome cowboy he'd dressed as tonight.

Needing a distraction from his nearness, she picked up his Stetson and set it on his head. "My mom's waiting for me outside."

He shot her a smile. "Can I take you out for coffee?"

"Are you trying to avoid my mother?"

"You bet."

Kayla laughed. She certainly didn't blame him. The last thing she wanted to do right now was tell her mother she'd just kissed Ty Lawrence. She had no idea what the future held, but for the moment she much preferred staying lost in his gaze. The details of what had transpired could be worked out later. "You didn't think I was going to leave you now, did you?"

"I hope not."

"You wait here, and I'll go tell her."

"No, I'll come with you."

She hurried outside with Ty at her side and headed toward the driver's side of the van, trying to calm the turmoil raging inside. Her mom wasn't going to respond well to this.

"Where have you been?" Her mom stuck her head out of the driver's window then frowned. "Ty? What are you doing here?"

"Mom." Kayla leaned her arm against the door and forced a smile. "Ty and I are going out for a cup of coffee. He'll drop me off later at my apartment."

"Kayla." Her mom grabbed Kayla's arm. "I need to talk to you. Alone."

Kayla glanced at Ty who looked as if he wished he were anywhere else but here. "Do you mind?"

He shook his head. "I'll go get my car."

Once he'd walked away, Kayla caught her mom's fiery gaze. "What is going on?"

Kayla kept her voice steady. "It's only coffee, Mom."

She wasn't ready to supply any further details. And besides, how could she when she didn't know exactly what had happened? One kiss might have left her head spinning, but the future still held no guarantees.

"Kayla, I thought you called things off with that man."

"He's not the same man he was a year ago."

"Apparently you're the same person." Her mother's frown deepened. "You haven't learned a thing."

Kayla stared at the side of the van and tried to control her temper. "Mom—"

"No. I want you to listen to me. Maybe you've forgotten, but the day you came back from Boston you were devastated. Ty Lawrence is a liar, and you know from the past that he will do anything to get what he wants. He's after you, Kayla, and if you don't turn and walk away right now, it's going to be too late."

Kayla clenched her hands until her fingernails bit into her palms. She forced herself to push away any lingering doubts of who Ty really was.

"A lot of things happened during this past year, Mom. Things that forced him to re-evaluate his life. I'm not saying we're getting back together, and I know you don't understand, but I believe him."

Her mom slammed her hands against the steering wheel. "Of course I don't understand. That is why I'm trying to stop you from making the biggest mistake of your life. You found out before it was too late last time, but this time. . ."

"Mom—"

"You're old enough to make your own decision, but don't ever come back to me and say I didn't warn you."

Kayla watched as her mom jerked the van into reverse and spun out of the parking lot. A moment later Ty pulled up beside her and reached over to open the passenger door. "Is everything all right?" he asked, as she climbed in beside him.

Kayla shook her head. "I knew she'd be upset, but she had so much hurt in her eyes. As if I let her down."

"Do you blame her?" Ty pulled out of the parking lot and headed for an all-night coffee shop around the corner. "She has no reason to believe me."

"You're not doing a very good job of convincing." Kayla laughed, but reality stung. While she might be old enough to make her own decisions, she still respected her mother's experienced opinion.

He reached out and squeezed her hand. "I was hoping I wouldn't have to convince you anymore."

"You don't. But she loves me and doesn't want me to get hurt."

Ty drove into a parking place and shut off the engine before turning to her. He pulled her hand toward his chest and caught her gaze. "I was a fool to lose you the last time, though I know I deserved it. I was never good enough for you."

Kayla struggled to take another breath. "That's not true—"

"Shhh." He pressed his finger against her lips. "Let me finish. I want to do things right this time, with everything out in the open. I am not perfect—you know that—but I promise you I will never intentionally hurt you again. Never."

She squeezed her arms around her waist and blinked back the tears. He was right about one thing. Ty *had* hurt her. He had deceived her. . .and yet she believed he was a changed man.

Oh God, please let me be right.

five

Yellow rays of afternoon sunlight filtered through the sheer living room curtains of Chloe Parker's house as Kayla emptied a box of crackers onto a glass plate. Smells of marinated steaks drifted in from the grill on the patio outside, mixing with the German potato salad and tangy coleslaw sitting on the antique mahogany table inside. As good as the spread looked, Kayla wasn't sure she'd be able to eat a single bite. Agreeing to bring Ty to dinner with her two best friends had been a step she'd undoubtedly jumped into sooner than she should have. How could she explain their relationship to her friends when she wasn't even ready to venture her own guess as to where they were headed? No matter what her heart wanted to believe, trust wasn't something that could be repaired overnight.

Chloe nudged Kayla with her elbow before shoving a strand of her long black hair out of her face. "I've yet to hear all the details behind how you and Ty got back together. Spill."

Kayla hesitated as she glanced around Chloe's cozy dining room that opened to the kitchen and living room. Black-and-white photos of her two small boys lined the fireplace mantel. A wooden box of toys sat in the corner of the room, beside a rocking chair that was the perfect size for two-year-old Brandon. Kayla pulled out some crab dip from the picnic basket she'd brought and set it on the table. A home and family were things she'd once planned to have with Ty. Losing that dream had shattered all her childhood illusions of living happily ever after. Having him back in her life had yet to erase the fears that her newfound hopes for the two of them might vanish a second time.

She drew in a breath and tried to calm the butterflies that flitted in her stomach. "There's honestly not much to tell at this point."

Chloe folded her arms across her chest. "Somehow I don't believe that."

"Me either." Jenny shook her head as she added a stack of paper plates from the kitchen bar to the buffet table. "You've been too hush-hush about everything. It's time you gave us a little insider information. We are your best friends, girl."

She couldn't help but laugh as she looked up at Chloe and Jenny who stood side by side like a pair of interrogation officers. She'd given them very few details during the past month, but that hadn't stopped them from arranging an afternoon barbeque where they could check out Ty for themselves.

Kayla tried to shrug off the ridiculous case of nerves that had consumed her all day. These were her friends. Best friends since the seventh grade when the three of them had stood up against Angie Edwards and the Farrington Junior High cheerleaders whose antics had put them at odds outside the classroom more than once.

Kayla gripped the edge of the table with her fingertips. "I promise I'm not trying to keep things from the two of you, but Ty and I still have a lot of things we need to work out. We're completely starting over."

"Right." Jenny's blue eyes widened. "And how long is that going to last?"

"Jenny." Kayla felt a blush cross her cheeks.

Ty's one kiss after the company-catered dinner and observing him when he didn't know she was there had managed to change her entire world and push aside the resolutions she'd put into place over the past year. But until all her doubts were gone she was determined they take things slowly. Which was exactly what had happened so far.

He'd kept his word, and they'd started seeing each other again as if they were dating for the first time. They'd gone out for dinner, movies at the Rialto Theater, ice cream at Barry's Café, and even a couple of Saturday afternoons on his friend Charlie's boat. In between they'd talked. She'd begun to trust him again—enough to let him into her life—but was still determined to move ahead with their relationship one slow step at a time. Which was exactly why she'd shared little with her mom—or with Jenny and Chloe—about their relationship.

"We're your friends." Jenny flung her arm around Kayla's shoulder. "All we want is what's best for you."

"Or perhaps a chance to check him out up close." Kayla shot her friend a grin as she picked up a serving spoon from the table and stuck it in the coleslaw.

"You bet that's what I mean." Jenny laughed, but her smile melted into a frown. "It's also our job to make sure you don't get your heart broken again."

The innocent comment pierced through the layer of protection Kayla had wrapped around her heart. She knew she had no guarantees Ty wouldn't walk off with the shattered pieces of her heart again. Kayla glanced out the kitchen window that overlooked the backyard and tried to ignore the implications. Ty stood beside the grill with the other two guys, looking as if he were having a good time. His white T-shirt showed off his tan skin, and when he laughed a dimple appeared on his left cheek. He'd always been irresistible. That's why she'd left Boston. Was she only fooling herself into believing things could be different this time around?

No. Things were different this time. Completely different. She was convinced of it.

"Jenny's exactly right, you know." Chloe interrupted Kayla's thoughts. "It's our job to watch out for each other."

"So what do you think about the new Ty?" Kayla dunked a cracker into the crab dip. Maybe food would settle her stomach after all.

Chloe picked up an empty sippy cup from the table then headed into the adjoining kitchen to rinse it out in the sink. "Honestly, while I'm happy for you, it's hard to be objective at this point. I mean, this is the guy who broke your heart, Kayla. I can't forget how many times you cried on my shoulder after you moved back."

"She is right, Kayla." Jenny popped open a jar of salsa and set it next to the chips. "I was supposed to be your maid of honor, and instead you came home with a broken heart."

Kayla frowned. The broken heart was one fact that no one, especially her mother, was willing to forget. And as many times as she'd tried to rationalize it, if she was honest with herself, it was an issue that was hard for her to leave in the past as well. "Things are different now."

"I hope so." Jenny followed Kayla's gaze out the window. "Though there never was any question as to how handsome the guy is."

"Don't let Greg hear you say that." Chloe laughed.

"What about your mom?" Jenny asked, ignoring Chloe's grin. "What does she think about him coming back into your life?"

"We don't talk about it." Kayla grabbed another cracker. "She'd like to pretend none of this is happening. She doesn't trust Ty at all."

"The steaks are done!" Chloe's husband, Nick, burst through the door interrupting any further conversation.

Chloe took the platter of meat from her husband to set on the table. "Are the kids behaving, honey?"

"Come look for yourself. Jeremy just roped Ty into a game of catch."

Chloe followed Nick outside with a clean plate for the grilled potatoes.

Kayla looked outside at the spacious backyard. It appeared that the game of catch had been postponed. At that moment four-year-old Jeremy was tackling Ty who was on his hands and knees. Two-year-old Brandon had hold of Ty's leg and was pulling with a determined look on his face.

A wave of peace flooded the corners of Kayla's heart as she watched the playful struggle until Ty collapsed to the ground, pretending to admit defeat.

"He's really good with kids," Jenny said, standing beside her.

"Funny thing is, I never knew it." Kayla watched Ty roll over and toss Brandon a foot into the air above him. "A year ago he wouldn't have been out there on the grass wrestling with two little boys. He'd have been too worried about messing up his designer suit."

"Can someone really change that much in such a short time?" Jenny laid her hand on Kayla's arm. "I'm sorry. I had no right—"

"It's okay." Hadn't she asked herself the very same question dozens of times over the past two weeks?

Jenny gave Kayla a hug. "I just don't want you to get hurt again."

Chloe set the potatoes on the table then rang the cast iron dinner bell to bring everyone to the table.

Thirty minutes later Ty leaned back and patted his firm

stomach. "Boy, am I full. This was delicious, ladies."

"Absolutely wonderful." Nick reached out and squeezed his wife's hand.

"I think it's time for two little boys to take a nap." Chloe looked at her kids whose eyes were beginning to droop.

Jeremy started to protest, but one look from his mother stopped him.

"Take a good nap for your mom, and I'll turn on the sprinkler later." Their father's offer brought smiles to their faces as they slid off their chairs and into his arms.

The scene brought a smile to Kayla's lips as well. She turned to Chloe. "You're lucky Nick's as good a father as he is a lawyer."

Five minutes later Nick returned from the boys' bedroom and came up behind Chloe to nuzzle his chin in her hair. "Are you into motorcycles, Ty?"

"I've ridden a few times." Ty set his fork down on the plate that had held the second piece of coconut pie Kayla had made. "My father had one when I was in high school—until he broke both legs and my mother made him sell it."

"Don't get any ideas." Nick covered Chloe's ears with his hands, a playful expression on his face. She squirmed out of his grasp before reaching up and planting a firm kiss on his lips.

"Good luck." Jenny reached out and grabbed Greg's hand. "I told Greg I'd never ride a motorcycle. Now he's got me outfitted with everything from a battery-heated vest to a pair of leather boots."

"We all know you're dying to check out Greg's new toy, so go have fun."

Chloe had barely finished her sentence when the men jumped up from the table. Nick kissed his wife again then headed for the garage door.

Kayla laughed, but a part of her still ached in confusion. A year ago holding hands or letting Ty kiss her had seemed a natural part of their relationship. Figuring out where they stood today was a whole other issue.

❧

Kayla let Ty take her hand and lead her down the tree-lined street in front of her apartment building. Walking through the quiet neighborhood was the perfect way to end the day.

"I like your friends." Ty kicked an acorn with the tip of his boot, then watched it bounce across the pavement.

"I'm glad." While she knew Chloe and Jenny still held a handful of reservations, the awkwardness of the day had melted into peacefulness as Kayla's friends had worked to make them both feel comfortable with a boisterous game of charades. "You sure seemed to enjoy Nick and Chloe's boys."

"They're sweet kids. It's been a long time since I had so much fun rolling on the grass."

"I don't think I've ever seen you roll on the grass." Kayla laughed. "I liked it."

"I guess you're right. A year ago I would have worried about what the next person might be thinking about me."

"And today?"

Ty stopped and turned so he could look at her.

"Only one person's opinion matters to me now." His blue eyes gazed at her.

"And whose is that?"

Ty tipped her chin and brought his face inches from Kayla's. "Yours."

Kayla could feel his warm breath on her face, but he made no move to lean down farther and kiss her. As much as she wanted his lips on hers, she took a step back. If she let him kiss her, she wouldn't be able to think clearly.

They started walking again in silence, each occupied with their own thoughts.

"Tell me what happened to Jack." It was the one subject they'd put off discussing. And one she needed to understand.

The muscles in his hand flinched, and she knew she'd broached a painful topic. Still, she had to know exactly what led Ty to change his life so drastically.

"I know this is a painful subject for you."

"And one you have every right to know." Ty led Kayla to a bench just off the road, under two large oak trees whose branches spanned the wide street. "Jack's death was a major factor in my finding Christ. It's sad, but in his death I found life."

"God's way of bringing good in the worst of circumstances?"

"Maybe." Ty was silent for a moment. "I'm not sure when Jack started having marital problems. He and his wife had been fighting for months, but shortly after you left Boston he found out Karen was having an affair with a man at her office."

"I'm sorry to hear that. Jack was a good guy."

"Within a week Karen filed the divorce papers and was gone. I never saw her again. Jack didn't take it well. I think deep down he honestly believed things would work out between them. When she didn't come back, it devastated him. Two weeks later I went by his apartment to pick him up for a basketball game. I found him lying dead on the kitchen floor. He'd shot himself."

Kayla shuddered and squeezed Ty's hand. "I'm so sorry."

"I'm sorry because Jack never knew God. He never knew Christ was the one place where he could have found relief and peace."

"What about you? How did his death change you?"

"My grandfather had a heart attack a month later. I was furious over losing you and then Jack. In a matter of a few weeks I'd lost everything that meant anything to me. It made me start thinking about what was important."

"What happened to your grandfather?"

"When he got out of the hospital he went into a retirement center. It wasn't what I wanted, but he insisted he didn't want to be a burden on anyone. I tried to visit him at least twice a week, sometimes more if my schedule allowed it. Soon I began to realize the things I had held important in my life weren't that important at all."

Kayla was silent as he continued.

"My grandfather never preached at me, but every time I came he asked me to read to him from the Bible. After a few weeks we had read through the Gospels, and I started asking questions. While the stories of Jesus and His life were not new to me, I had missed the message of the tremendous love behind them: The love of a Savior willing to come to this earth and die for me of all people. I found it hard to believe."

"So what changed your mind?"

"I started thinking about Jack who believed he had nothing to live for, and I wondered very seriously what I had to live for. My job was unfulfilling, and the more hours I put into work, the more resentful I became. What was the point in working twelve to fourteen hours a day, seven days a week? Life seemed meaningless."

"Didn't Solomon write that everything is meaningless?" Kayla fumbled with the shiny red stones on her charm bracelet and pondered her own question.

Ty nodded. " 'To the man who pleases him, God gives wisdom, knowledge and happiness, but to the sinner he gives the task of gathering and storing up wealth to hand it over to the one who pleases God. This too is meaningless, a chasing after the wind.'

"I found that verse at one point, and it struck me so that I memorized it. That's what my life had become. One meaningless day after another, I was chasing after the wind and finding nothing. It took me sinking into the depths to realize I was a sinner who needed a Savior."

Kayla looked up at him, her eyes swelling with tears of joy. "I'm glad, Ty. I'm so glad."

"For the first time I saw a light at the end of the tunnel. I went to the minister of a friend I knew, and he studied with me. It still took a while to get through my hard head, but finally I saw the truth. I realized the only way I could live was if I died to my sinful nature. I accepted Christ and was baptized one glorious Sunday afternoon. My grandfather died last January. I think he'd been waiting for me to get my life turned around."

"I wish you would have called me."

He looked at her and caught her gaze. "Before you left I promised you I would stay out of your life. I wasn't ready to see you until I had worked through some things. I actually never planned to come here, but I also know it's not a coincidence I'm here."

For the first time in a long while Kayla smiled at the future.

&

Richard Abbott threw the rest of his corned beef sandwich into the trash and ran his fingers through his thinning hair. He hadn't left his office in three days, and he was running out of time. Rumors of indictments were getting closer and felt like a noose closing in around his neck. He picked up a file filled with Ty Lawrence's signatures. There was, according to his lawyer, a way out. Now it was only a matter of time before putting things into motion. The way Lawrence walked out on him was something he'd never forgive. He once trusted him, priming him to become his right-hand man. And for what? It didn't really matter anymore. Because Ty Lawrence, former protégé, was going to take the fall for him.

six

Ty tapped his finger against the steering wheel and glanced at the rearview mirror. A black sedan swung into the turning lane and stopped three cars behind him. He stared at the red light. He'd noticed the same car in the parking lot at work. And at the gas station where he'd just filled up his car.

His jaw muscles tightened. He'd caught today's headlines from the newsstand five minutes ago. The investigation of Abbott Financial Services made for a riveting front-page story. Not unexpected, but disturbing nevertheless. He might believe Abbott deserved to spend the rest of his life behind bars, but his downfall would affect hundreds of employees if the company ended up filing for bankruptcy.

He punched the speed dial number for his former secretary into his speakerphone, hoping to catch her at home. She answered on the third ring.

"Penny here."

"Penny, it's Ty." The light turned green, and he pushed on the accelerator to make the left turn.

"Ty?" The line was silent for a moment. "What a nice surprise."

"Did you get the flowers I sent you?"

"They were beautiful, though you didn't have to."

"After all you did for me the past five years, a bunch of flowers seems to pale in comparison."

"You're right about that."

Penny chuckled, and Ty remembered why he liked her.

She'd always been efficient and dependable with an added sense of humor.

"Still finding time to sail?"

Ty paused at her question as he checked the rearview mirror again. If only he were out sailing right now instead of being tossed into the middle of some criminal investigation. The black sedan had fallen back into the light five o'clock traffic but was still there. He shot into the left-hand lane before turning onto a residential street to test his theory.

"Sailing? Yeah. A couple of times on my friend's boat, the *Angelina*." He swallowed hard as the other car turned, still on his trail. "How are things at work?"

"Not much has changed. Mr. Abbott's been staying out of sight. The government officially opened up their investigation into the company yesterday."

"I saw the headlines."

"You'll be on the short list of people they want to question."

Ty frowned. "Thanks for the encouragement."

"On the bright side everyone misses you."

"I don't think that piece of information will impress the government." Ty took another sharp left through a stop sign. The sedan shot straight ahead. He felt himself relax. Either they knew he was on to them, or his imagination was working overtime. Of course, there had been other incidents he'd tried to dismiss as coincidence. Misplaced files at the office. The sense that someone had gone through his desk at home. He shook his head. Surely it was nothing. He'd never been someone to overreact in a challenging situation, and he wasn't sure what had him keyed up tonight. The whole idea that someone was after him seemed ridiculous.

He took another sharp left and headed back to the main street. "What's the news from the inside?"

"So far no one's been arrested, so we're all holding our breath and hoping it'll all disappear."

Ty shook his head. That was exactly what Abbott wanted to happen. Cover his tracks well enough, and he'd get the money and the company. Unless he and his dirty lawyers managed to pin the indictment on someone else. "You should leave. I could look into getting you a job here."

"Thanks, but I've decided to stick it out. If the company goes down, which I'm hoping it won't, I won't have lost anything. And it's not that bad. I'd never make this much money in Farrington."

"Trust me, Penny. Money's not always worth the price."

"So you've always tried to tell me. Hey. Before you hang up, how are your parents? Are they back in Massachusetts for the summer?"

"They actually decided to stay in Florida this year. Apparently they're loving every minute of retirement."

"I would have enjoyed seeing them again."

"Me, too." Ty chuckled. "They haven't been up here for months."

"Be sure to tell them hello for me when you see them."

"I will. And, Penny, be careful. I don't trust Abbott. He'll sacrifice the company and all its employees in a second to save his own hide."

"Don't forget I'm a big girl, Ty. I can take care of myself."

"I hope so."

After saying good-bye Ty hung up, wishing he could simply erase the past five years of his life. He might have left without any illegal involvement, but the truth could easily be twisted and misconstrued. Something at which Abbott was far too proficient.

Not only did this leave his new position vulnerable, but his future with Kayla was at stake. Giving her a reason not to trust him was something he couldn't let happen, and an indictment would come with rumors of corruption and fraud. Ty gripped the steering wheel as he pulled into the parking lot of his apartment building. Richard Abbott had nothing on him. Which meant that all he could do now was pray things stayed that way.

⋙

Kayla grabbed the schedule from the color printer in her mom's office and handed a copy to the older woman. "It's going to be a busy week. Three business dinners, a birthday lunch for fifty, and a retirement party."

"Guess we can handle that." Her mom studied the details before sliding it into a clear binder. "Where are you off to in such a hurry?"

Kayla wished she could have avoided the question but knew it was pointless. "Ty and I are taking Chloe's boys to the zoo in Plymouth for the day."

A shadow crossed her mother's face. "So you're still going out with Ty."

Somehow she'd managed to avoid the topic, which in turn had guaranteed any arguments had been dodged as well. But as her relationship with Ty grew she couldn't avoid the reality that if things continued the way they were, she'd be planning a wedding in the coming months. "I know you don't like him, but—"

"You're right. I don't like him—" Her mom flicked the binder onto the desk before setting her fists on her hips. "—or trust him or want him in your life."

Kayla grabbed her notebook and purse, then started to leave. She'd never win a round head-on with her mom in this arena. The woman was simply too stubborn. "Mom, I don't want to get into this."

Her mom grasped Kayla's forearm, stopping her in the doorway. "Honey, I'm your mother and I love you, but you're setting yourself up again. You can't believe him."

Kayla worked to control her rising frustration. "But I do believe him, and as much as you don't want me to, nothing is going to change that."

The past few weeks had given Kayla more than enough time to see for herself that Ty was truly a changed man. And while they were still taking things slow with their relationship, the fear that had plagued Kayla for so long was finally beginning to disappear.

From her mother's cold expression, Kayla knew nothing she might say would be enough to convince the older woman of Ty's newfound virtues.

Her mom's grip strengthened on her arm. "I think it's time I told you exactly why I feel so strongly about Ty Lawrence. Then I promise never to bring it up again."

Kayla's brow furrowed. It wasn't like her mother to make emotional deals. She glanced at her watch. Ty was meeting her at Chloe's in thirty minutes, giving her little time to get ready. But one look at her mother's pained expression and she knew she owed her the respect to at least listen. She followed her mother into the country-style living room and sat across from her on the pale blue couch.

Her mom tucked an auburn strand of her hair back into the clasp it had fallen from then scooted forward on the cushion. "Your father swept me off my feet the first time I saw him. He was charming, sincere, and everything I'd ever dreamed of. When we got married I had such high hopes for our lives together. He had a good job working in management for a local grocery store, and I planned to stay home and have babies."

Kayla saw the silent quiver of pain reflected in her mother's eyes as she spoke and felt her heart break.

"After we had been married a few years, everything began to change. He lost his job and started drinking. I was so blinded by what I wanted to believe until it was too late." Her mom reached out and grasped Kayla's hands. "But it's not too late for you, Kayla. You know Ty is a manipulator and a liar. He's out to win you no matter what it takes, and after he does, then you won't matter to him anymore. You're like a trophy he's set on winning, and once he does he'll be free to go on to bigger and better prizes."

Kayla flicked at her broken thumbnail as she struggled with how to respond to her mother's pain without negating it. Her mother's harsh view of men had always stemmed from her own experiences. That she knew. But that assessment didn't have to include Ty. At least not the man Ty had become.

"I know you're concerned about me, Mom, and you have every right to be. But you haven't been around Ty lately. He's not the same man."

"People don't change, Kayla. Not really." Her mom reached up to rub the back of her neck and looked intently at her daughter. "I'd love to tell you it's possible for Ty to have changed into some knight in shining armor and the two of you are going to live happily ever after, but that would take a miracle. This is real life where more often than not, the prince fools around with his secretary or gets himself killed over a six-pack of beer."

Her mom was silent for a moment as tears welled in the corners of her eyes. "Just think about what I told you and please, please, be careful."

"You know I will."

Kayla leaned over and kissed her mom's cheek. Her heart

ached for her mother, whose dreams of happiness had been shattered by one man's choices. Even after twenty-three years the pain still refused to leave. But Kayla believed in miracles. And Ty Lawrence wasn't her father. As far as she was concerned, he'd already proven it.

a.

"I can't remember the last time I went to the zoo." Ty handed Brandon a bag of popcorn, not even attempting to hide his boyish enthusiasm. "Are you sure you don't want one?"

"I'm sure." Kayla chuckled as she pushed the stroller past the food kiosk and toward the monkeys. Summer was dwindling to an end, but the day was still warm and sunny. "The real question is, are you sure you're going to survive putting up with two preschoolers for the rest of the morning?"

"Are you kidding?" Ty ruffled the top of Jeremy's hair. "They're adorable."

"He sure has latched onto you."

Ty had begged to come along after Kayla had promised Chloe she would watch Brandon and Jeremy for the morning. So far things were working out great. Jeremy had already found a best buddy in Ty and had attached himself to his side. Brandon was content to ride in the stroller Chloe had provided.

Ty scooped Jeremy in his arms and lifted him onto his shoulders as they stopped in front of the chimpanzees. Kayla smiled at the father and son impression. It wasn't hard to picture her and Ty, five years from now, with a couple of children in tow.

Unless her mother's concerns were valid.

"Kayla?"

Ty's voice broke into her thoughts, and she tried to shove the unwanted assumption aside. But her mother hadn't been the only one to plant seeds of doubt in her mind. Jenny and Chloe were still just as upfront with their reservations. It was going to take much more than a free morning of babysitting to convince her best friends Ty no longer had an ulterior motive rolled up the sleeve of his pinstriped suit.

"Are you all right?" Ty nudged her with his elbow as she pushed the stroller up the slight incline. "You've been awfully quiet."

"I'm fine." She smiled, irritated at herself for letting other people's biased opinions affect her. Ty deserved her trust. They stopped in front of a family of monkeys lying in the sun behind the glass barrier.

"I saw a big front page write-up on Abbott Financial Services in the headlines. Looks like it's a good thing you got out when you did. Possible indictments, arrests. . ." She saw a shadow cross his face and realized it was probably a topic he'd prefer to avoid. Especially if he knew some of those who might be involved. At least she knew he was innocent. Ty might not have always been on the up-and-up with her in the past, but he wasn't a thief. "I'm sorry. I—"

"No. It's fine. I told you one of the reasons I left was that some unscrupulous things were going on."

"So you think Abbott's guilty?" she asked as they started walking toward the next exhibit. "The article quoted him as defending himself, but the report implied the missing funds were an inside job."

"I want some ice cream." Jeremy's chubby fingers grabbed at Ty's hair.

"Ice cream?" Ty seemed to latch onto the change of subject. "You can't be hungry."

Kayla's eyes widened in amusement, Ty's old employer quickly forgotten. "You've got a handful of popcorn in your hand, and you want ice cream?"

"Yes!" Ty and Jeremy said in unison.

Kayla just shook her head and glanced down at Brandon who lay sound asleep in his stroller beneath the warm sunshine.

"Hurry up!" Kayla laughed at the enthusiastic expression on Ty's face and wondered how she could even think about doubting him. "The rest of the zoo is waiting for us."

Two hours later Kayla spread out a sheet on the picnic table and began to unload the lunch they'd brought. It seemed the ice cream and other goodies picked up along the way had not diminished the appetites of Jeremy and Ty. Even Brandon was awake and ready for his share.

As Kayla passed out peanut butter and jelly sandwiches with apple slices and carrot sticks, she asked Jeremy what his favorite part of the morning had been so far. The four-year-old hesitated only briefly before deciding that petting the goats had been the best part.

"What about me?" Ty shot her a dejected look.

"What was your favorite part?" Kayla asked obligingly.

Ty cocked his head and looked deeply into Kayla's eyes. "Being with you."

"Isn't that kind of sappy?" Kayla managed a chuckle, but her breath caught in her throat.

"What can I say? I'm in love."

Kayla froze for a moment, then turned to look out across the green lawn bordered with orange and yellow flowers. Her heart battled with the noise of common sense that seemed to assail her at every turn from well-meaning friends and family members. She loved Ty. That had never been an issue. But reestablishing a broken relationship didn't come with a handbook. At the moment she didn't know if she was ready for the next step. She had to come to the point where she trusted him completely no matter what anyone else said. That was the only way their relationship would ever work.

"I'm sorry." Ty tossed the rest of his sandwich into the picnic basket.

She reached out and squeezed his hand. "It's not you."

"You're not thinking of breaking things off, are you?"

She shook her head and ignored the warnings that continued to surface.

"Kayla, if I'm going too fast I'll slow down." Ty picked a piece of grass at the edge of the blanket and rolled it between his fingers. "You don't trust me yet, do you?"

"I trust you." She wiped a tear that slid down her cheek, wishing she didn't feel so emotional. "But I can't forget how hurt I was when I found out the truth. I don't ever want to go through that again."

Kayla sat silent for a moment, searching for the right words.

"And I talked to my mother this morning." She handed Brandon his sippy cup. "Or shall I say my mother talked to me."

"I can just imagine how that conversation went. It's not a secret she can't stand me."

"She says it's impossible for someone to change as you claim you have. It would take a miracle, were her exact words, I believe."

"It did take a miracle."

She looked up and caught his gaze. "I know, Ty, but religious transformations don't impress my mother."

"What do you believe? Because that's all I care about. I told you from the very beginning that if you told me to walk out of your life and never come back I would respect your wishes. But that's not what I want to happen."

She blinked back the tears. "I don't want you to walk out of my life."

Ty laced his fingers with hers, the two little ones forgotten for the moment. "As long as we're honest with each other, Kayla, we'll make this relationship work."

❧

"How were the boys today?" Chloe plopped herself down on Kayla's couch with a bowl of potato chips, ready for their monthly Friday night girls' time. Pizza and junk food were the standard fare along with heart-to-heart chats that often lasted into the early hours of the morning.

"Your kids were adorable." Kayla tossed Chloe an extra pillow then checked her watch. Jenny was predictably late. "You can imagine how excited they were when they got to feed the giraffe."

"I understand that finally beat out feeding the goat on the excitement scale." Chloe picked up the rolled newspaper Kayla had left on the lounge chair earlier and popped off the rubber band. "Is this today's paper?"

"Yes. I haven't even had a chance to look at it."

Kayla ducked back into the kitchen to grab the rest of the snacks she'd whipped together this afternoon. Seven-layer dip with corn chips for Chloe. Chocolate chip cookies for Jenny. When Kayla returned, Chloe was busy scouring the entertainment section.

"Nick's sister is writing a sort of 'Dear Abby' column for the *Farrington Chronicle* now." Chloe flipped back to the front page. "By the way. What company did Ty work for in Boston?"

"Abbott Financial Services."

"There's an article in here about them."

"They've been in the paper a lot lately. The government is investigating the company." Kayla set the food on the coffee table. "What does that article say?"

"Police brought a man here in Farrington in for questioning last night regarding an estimated $175 million believed to be missing."

"Someone here in Farrington?"

"They're trying to prove the books have been altered for the past few years. Ty worked with finances?"

Kayla shot a piece of popcorn at Chloe, hitting her target. She didn't like the obvious conclusion. "Don't start with this again. I know for a fact that Ty wasn't at the police department last night."

"Had a hot date?"

Kayla's stomach knotted. "Actually, no. He cancelled. Some emergency came up at work, and he had to stay late."

Chloe didn't have to say anything for Kayla to know what her friend was thinking. Kayla stared out the window overlooking the apartment's manicured lawns. She still believed he may have lied to her in the past, but even the old Ty wouldn't have done anything illegal like embezzle a fortune.

Chloe folded up the paper and set it down. "Don't worry. I may not completely trust Ty, but even I can't see him involved in a fraud case."

"Of course he wouldn't be." Kayla pushed aside any doubts that were rising to the surface. The whole thought of Ty being a thief was. . .ridiculous. "If Ty said he was at work, then that's where he was."

As long as we're honest with each other.

Kayla shook her head. "The article doesn't matter. I have chosen to trust Ty. If he needs to tell me something, then he will."

The doorbell rang, and Kayla jumped up from the couch to get the pizza she'd ordered.

As long as we're honest with each other. As long as we're honest.

seven

Three weeks later Kayla hurried up the stairs to her apartment, wondering how Ty could have forgotten his wallet in her apartment. She'd cleaned up the living room last night and didn't remember seeing it anywhere. Normally he was the organized one in contrast to her typically chaotic routine. Something she knew annoyed Ty no end. She could pull off a five-course dinner for twelve in her sleep, but forget trying to keep a balanced checkbook or her tax information up-to-date. She was every accountant's nightmare. And the reason she'd had to hire one herself.

She fumbled to find her keys in her purse.

Ty moved in beside her, casting a shadow over her purse. "Can I help?"

Kayla laughed and scooted him aside with her hip. "Your wallet's not going anywhere, and trust me, you don't want to stick your hand in here."

Ty leaned against the doorframe, waiting until she finally was able to swing open the door.

"Happy Birthday!"

The handle of the door hit the wall with a thud. Kayla jumped. A dozen of her friends stood beneath a long banner in her living room, announcing in bold letters that today she turned thirty.

Ty entered the room behind her, ducking to avoid a tangle of balloons and streamers that skimmed the ceiling. "Are you surprised?"

"Surprised? I had no idea!" Kayla smiled at Chloe, Jenny, and some of her other friends from church. "And Ty's wallet?"

"All a ruse." Chloe stepped forward to give her friend a hug. "We just wanted to remind you that your twenty-something years are over. It's a new decade for you, sister."

"She's right." Jenny stepped up and wrapped an arm around Kayla's shoulder. "And you know what happens when you hit thirty."

Kayla placed her hands on her hips and quirked an eyebrow at her friend. "Since you're already there, I am sure you'll have lots of advice."

"Very funny." Jenny laughed then waved her hands at the guests.

Kayla greeted everyone as she made her way to her dining room table. "Mom. The cake is beautiful." Kayla hugged her mother who stood beside the table, thankful they'd chosen simple pink roses rather than a black, over-the-hill theme. "And you actually kept this from me."

Her mom's grin widened. "Trust me—it wasn't easy."

"It never has been, has it? I still remember two or three surprise parties you tried to throw me as a child. Somehow I always found out."

Ty scooted up beside Kayla and laughed. "I knew there had to be a devious streak running through you."

The smile on her mother's lips vanished as she excused herself to pour a glass of punch on the other side of the table.

Ty nudged Kayla with his elbow. "I wasn't trying to offend her."

"Don't worry about it."

Kayla frowned, wishing she could take her own advice. Why couldn't the two people she loved most in the world get along?

Chloe cut the cake while Jenny served the punch and passed it out to the guests. Once everyone was served, Chloe motioned toward the others in the room. "Since everyone has cake now, why don't you all sit down? Kayla, we chipped in and got you a little something."

Jenny handed her the gift.

"You guys are too sweet." Kayla set her cake plate down and ripped open the foil wrapping paper to reveal a brand new food processor.

"You needed a new one," Chloe said, collecting the used paper. "It seemed like the perfect gift."

"This is great. All except the fact that I'm thirty now. I was hoping to forget that tiny detail."

Ty slid in between Kayla and Jenny on the couch, and she caught her mom's disapproving frown across the room. Somehow Kayla was going to have to find a way for a truce.

"To Kayla." Ty held up his cup of punch. "To the best girl a guy could ever find."

"Then let's just hope she finds the right guy." Her mother's cold words seemed to hover in the room before she stood and stalked toward the kitchen.

No one spoke. The tension in the air squeezed at Kayla's chest. She glanced at Ty, wishing she could erase the hurt in his eyes. . .and the disappointment in her mother's.

"I'm sorry. I'll. . ." Kayla stood, not knowing what to do. Talking to her mother would do little to change the situation. "Please, everyone. There's plenty of cake. Eat up."

Kayla made a hasty exit into the kitchen to find her mom. The chocolate cake she'd just finished soured in her stomach. Somehow she would have to find a way to bring out the white flag and form a truce between Ty and her mom— before Ty decided Boston wasn't so bad after all.

Her mother leaned against the counter with her hands gripping her temples. She'd aged the past few years, and while she still had the energy of someone a decade or so younger, life had left its mark in the creases of her face.

"You had no right to say that, Mom." Kayla folded her arms across her chest and bit back the sharp words she wanted to spout out. "No matter what you think about Ty, he doesn't deserve to be humiliated in front of all my friends."

"Really?" Her mother shook her head. "Well, someone in this family needs to hold on to a little bit of common sense because you don't have any left."

"Because I love Ty?" Kayla squelched the urge to scream. "You don't get it, do you?"

"Get what?"

"The fact that I'm old enough to make my own decisions on who I let into my life."

Her mom fell back against the counter and continued to press her fingertips against her forehead.

A wave of concern took precedence over her frustration. "Are you having another one of your headaches, Mom?"

"Yes, but it's nothing."

Kayla started digging through one of the upper cabinets for a bottle of painkillers before handing her mom two of the pills. "I need you to accept him as part of my life."

The older woman turned to face her daughter. "Maybe when you have your own children someday you'll understand what I'm going through. Kayla, I watched that man lie to you and hurt you, and I don't want it to happen again."

Kayla winced at her mother's pointed words. "It's not going to. If you would take the time to get to know Ty, you would see he's not the same person he was a year ago."

"He's a charmer, Kayla. He knows how to get what he wants.

How is that any different from a year ago?"

Kayla bit her lip. It was useless trying to get her mother to understand. "You're just going to have to trust me."

"I trust you. That's not the problem. The problem is that I don't trust him. What about the government's investigation into the company he used to work for? Have you stopped to consider he could be part of it? I don't want you to go through the pain you went through all over again."

"Ty's not involved." Kayla braced her arms against the counter and shook her head. "I don't know what to say, except that I'm a grown woman. If I'm wrong about Ty, which I know I'm not, I'm the one who will have to live with the consequences."

Her mother caught her gaze and frowned. "And that's exactly what I'm afraid of."

&

Two hours later Ty poured himself a cup of water from the sink, certain he'd somehow misunderstood Kayla's last comment. "You want me to go to dinner with you and your mother?"

Kayla folded her arms across her chest and frowned. "You sound as if I'm asking you to steal England's crown jewels for me."

He rubbed the back of his neck and tried to put a check on his frustration. A showdown with Mrs. Marceilo was one of the inevitable factors in his relationship with Kayla, but he hadn't expected to end today with having to eat dinner with the woman. That would simply push them into round two. And the possibility of winning the affections of Rosa Marceilo was about as likely as his being called by NASA to oversee their next mission to Mars. Impossible.

Besides, he'd been looking forward to a quiet dinner at the Blue Moon to celebrate Kayla's birthday—with reservations for two. There had to be a way out of this one. "You know your mother hates me, and—"

"She doesn't hate you." Kayla patted his arm and offered him a smile. "She just doesn't. . .like you."

He dumped the rest of his water into the sink, his appetite for tonight's dinner suddenly diminished. "What's the difference?"

"Come on, Ty." She grabbed her purse and car keys off the kitchen's laminated countertop. "The two of you need to get to know each other."

"And you really think this is a good idea?"

"If you see our relationship heading forward, then yes." Her eyes flashed an angry warning. "She's my mother, and you can't blame her for not trusting you. She loves me."

Ty took a step backward and bumped against the counter. *What was this? Accept my mother or you're history?* Now it was his turn to feel the anger swell in his chest. This ultimatum sat about as well as the proposed dinner with her mom. Why did her mom have to be part of the package anyway? His parents were perfectly content to let Ty live his own life and rarely, if ever, butted in on his relationships. While he could understand the woman's hesitations over his past, he was tired of having to prove himself.

"I told her we would pick her up after everyone left." Kayla slung her purse strap onto her shoulder and softened her expression. "Please, Ty. For me?"

It wasn't fair. He'd rather she had asked him to steal the crown jewels. Going to dinner with the woman who'd just cut him down in front of Kayla's friends was asking too much.

He shoved his hands into his pockets, realizing he had little choice in the matter. "I'll go, but know that I'm doing this under protest."

With a nod, Kayla grabbed her purse and followed him out

the door before locking it behind her. He took a deep breath as they hurried down the sidewalk and worked to crush his growing frustration. Proving to Kayla he'd changed had been tough enough, albeit necessary. Having to do the same with her mom and friends was enough to make him doubt he'd ever find true acceptance in her life again.

Still, if he was honest with himself, it wasn't Kayla's fault her mother felt the way she did. And besides, what was one lousy dinner in the scope of things? At least Kayla would be happy. Maybe it wasn't asking too much for him to make a concerted effort.

"I have a birthday present for you." He opened the passenger door to let her into the car, determined to shake the dark mood that had come between them.

She hesitated before getting in. "Does that mean you've forgiven me for asking—"

"Insisting."

"Okay. For insisting you have dinner with my mom?"

"Not necessarily." He shot her a grin, then hurried around to the driver's seat. "Just remember—they say good things come in small packages."

Reaching into the glove compartment, he pulled out a red envelope and handed it to her.

Kayla ripped into the envelope and took out a pair of tickets. "We're going to the symphony?"

"In Boston."

Her face broke into a smile. "Do you know how long it's been since I've gone to a concert? This is wonderful!"

"I thought you might like a nice evening to dress up. Dinner's included."

"Thank you." Kayla turned to him, her face hovering inches from his.

Ty swallowed hard as he breathed in the sweetness of her perfume. As hard as it had been, he'd respected her wishes to take things slow, but starting over had proven far more difficult than he'd imagined. His heart had never let go. Unable to stop himself, he cupped her chin in his hand and reached over to kiss her. His heart pounded as he responded to her nearness, but the promise to let her set the pace convicted him.

He pulled back. "I'm sorry—"

"No. I'm sorry."

His heart sank at her declaration. He tried to read her expression, but all he could see were the tears welling in her eyes. "For kissing me?"

"No. I shouldn't have put you in such an awkward position tonight." She ran her thumb down his cheek and smiled. "Maybe I'm the one who doesn't deserve you."

"No. That's definitely my role." He breathed out a sigh of relief, reminded of all the reasons he'd decided that winning her back was worth it. He needed Kayla in his life, and if that meant including her mother, then so be it. "Then I'm not sorry for kissing you, but I am sorry for hassling you over dinner with your mom."

"You're forgiven, but that doesn't change the fact that I need you to make an effort with my mother."

"Make an effort?" *Whose side was she on?* "I'm not the one who stood in front of a roomful of people this afternoon and tried to humiliate your mother. If I remember correctly she's the one who keeps pulling all the punches."

"Ty."

"What? I'm willing to make peace, but she's got to be open to the idea as well."

"You can't make an effort by behaving as if she doesn't

exist." Kayla shoved the tickets into her purse, then snapped it shut. "I'll call her and tell her we're on our way."

Ty pulled onto Cranberry Highway, wondering, as he was with Abbott Financial, if a bomb weren't about to explode.

❧

The phone rang a half dozen times, then switched to the answering machine. Strange. Her mother had said she was going straight home. She bit her lip and stared at her cell phone.

"What's wrong?"

Kayla shrugged. "Nothing. I just don't know why she doesn't answer. She told me she was going straight home."

"The ringer could be off, she could be taking a shower. . . there are tons of reasons why she's not answering her phone."

She dropped her phone into her purse, still irritated at Ty's lack of enthusiasm to meet her mother halfway. She was getting tired of playing referee between two adults. "You're probably right, but she had another bad headache today. I'm worried about her."

Ty drove through the tree-lined streets that led to her mom's house, then pulled into the driveway. Her mom's car was parked by the garage door.

"I'll be right back." Kayla unlocked the door and jumped out of the car.

Ty was right behind her. "I'm coming with you."

Kayla hurried up the winding brick path, trying to get rid of the nagging feeling in the pit of her stomach that something was wrong. Shivering from the cool, fall breeze, she rang the bell several times before scrambling for her key in her purse so she could open the door.

"Mom?" She stepped into the three-bedroom home.

Mail was strewn across the floor of the normally tidy

entryway. A sweater lay in a pile on the floor beside it, instead of on the coat rack.

"Mom?" She walked through the kitchen, then rushed down the hall.

Kayla froze in the doorway of the master bedroom. Her mother lay face down beside the bed.

eight

Kayla felt her lungs constrict. Her mother's hands lay beside the green comforter that had slid onto the floor. Blood trickled from her forehead, staining the beige carpet. Ty gripped Kayla's elbow, but she couldn't move. She'd let her mom leave the party with an ultimatum that she accept Ty into her life, or else. Or else what? She had no right to speak to her mother that way... and now she lay unconscious on the floor. If she died...

Ty knelt beside her mom. "She's breathing, Kayla."

She tried to swallow the knot of fear—and guilt—that rose in her throat. "She told me she was dizzy, and all I did was give her some pain medicine. I should have noticed something was wrong."

"There's no way you could have known, sweetie. I'm calling 911." Ty pulled his cell phone from his back pocket and flipped it open. "It's going to be okay."

Kayla fell to her knees beside her mother. *It's going to be okay. It's going to be okay....* Ty was right. An ambulance would come to take her mom to the hospital. They'd run some tests, and in the end everything would be all right. Fifty-three was too young to die.

"Mom?" She pushed away the blood-stained strands of hair that stuck to her cheek. The left side of her face drooped, and drool ran down the edges of her mouth. How long had her mom been lying here?

Ty's voice and the rest of the bedroom faded into the background.

There was no response. No acknowledgment of Kayla's presence. Only the slight rise and fall of her chest beneath her flowered blouse.

Kayla tried to steady her own ragged breathing. "It's going to be all right, Mom. I'm here."

"Kayla?" Ty crouched beside her to wipe away her tears with his thumbs. She'd been crying and didn't even know it. "I'm going to wait outside for the ambulance. Are you going to be all right if I leave you for a few minutes?"

Kayla nodded then gripped his shoulder. "I'm scared, Ty."

"Your mom's too stubborn to let something like this get the best of her." He tilted up her chin with his fingertips and caught her gaze. "With the Lord's help we'll get through this, Kayla. I promise."

ఓ

Twenty minutes later Ty pulled his car out of the driveway behind the ambulance and followed it down the highway toward town. Rows of trees had already begun to turn from summer's shades of green into their yearly fall array of scarlet, orange, and yellow. In a few short weeks piles of fat pumpkins would lie for sale in front of the farms, and the cranberry bogs would be flooded in order to harvest the crimson fruit. But instead of enjoying the scenic drive the landscape blurred before him.

He reached over and took Kayla's hand, pulling it to his chest. "I'm sorry, Kayla. I know how close you are to your mother."

Kayla stared off into the distance. "I never thought of her getting sick. Not yet anyway. She's my mother, invincible and timeless."

"Don't give up yet." He squeezed her hand, wishing he could do more than simply offer words of encouragement.

"She's strong. With your help—with our help and the Lord's—she'll pull through this."

"I should have seen something was wrong."

Ty thumped the palm of his hand against the steering wheel, understanding far too well the intense feelings of regret. "You have to let it go, Kayla. The last thing your mother needs right now is for you to beat yourself up because you missed something that wasn't there. She's going to have her own battle to win, and you'll have to be there for her 100 percent."

"I know. It's just weird all that goes through your mind at a time like this." She glanced at him as he crossed an intersection behind the ambulance. "Nothing's ever going to be the same again, is it?"

"Probably not."

Life was good at bringing unanticipated changes. Something he'd seen far too often in his own life. Sometimes it threw a curve ball—like Kayla calling off their engagement. Only God could have taken that situation and brought good out of it a year later. There had been plenty of other unexpected twists, like finding out his mentor and boss was a man with no scruples and even fewer morals.

"Kayla, I'm sorry about something else. I should have given your mother a chance. I wasn't the one to forgive, and I haven't been much of an example."

"I know, more than anyone else, how difficult she can be. I just wanted things to work out between the two of you, and now. . ." She looked down and fiddled with her purse strap. "Ty, she doesn't believe in God. She told me once she'd seen too much pain and heartache in her life—in this world—to justify the existence of a God. And if He did exist, she didn't want anything to do with Him."

The feeling was uncomfortably familiar. How many times had he told God he'd never believe because a good God wouldn't leave a child to starve in Somalia or let things like 9/11 happen? He'd finally realized he'd been blaming God for man's choices. Not that it made things any easier.

"I guess your mother and I have more in common than I realized. For too long I tried to make God into what I wanted. Problem is, I found out He doesn't work that way. Man wants a God who will fulfill their desires and leave them feeling like they're in charge. Instead Jesus calls us to take up our cross and follow Him."

"That's pretty profound, isn't it?"

They were both quiet for a moment as he followed the ambulance toward the hospital. God wasn't a deity to be put into a box and brought out like a genie in a lamp. He'd learned that lesson all too well. Following Jesus called for a full-time commitment. No one said that taking up a cross was going to be easy. It was something he was still trying to get right.

Kayla looked over at him. "What if it's too late? I'm not ready to lose her."

Ty turned the corner into the hospital parking lot and for the first time in his life prayed for Rosa Marceilo.

❧

Ty stood in the doorway of the third-floor hospital room and watched Kayla sleep. The padded chair looked anything but comfortable. Just like the lump that had lodged in his throat and wouldn't go away. The MRI had confirmed a stroke, and while it was possible she would fully recover, Rosa Marceilo's life and that of her daughter had more than likely changed forever.

Kayla opened her eyes, then slowly sat up to stretch her back. "I hadn't planned to fall asleep."

"I went for a walk." He pulled the other chair up beside her. "I knew you were tired and didn't want to wake you. How is she?"

"She woke up a little while ago, confused but thankfully calm when I told her what had happened. I'm hoping she'll sleep through the rest of the night." Kayla stifled a yawn. "What time is it?"

"Ten thirty." He held up the boxed dinner. "Are you hungry? I brought you a sandwich. All they had left at the deli was tuna fish."

Kayla looked at the box of hospital food and wrinkled her nose. "I'm sorry. You're sweet, but I don't think I can handle fish right now."

"We could try the cafeteria if they're open." Ty dumped the box on the chair beside him when she didn't respond. "How are you doing?"

"I'm still in a daze. I just can't believe all this is happening. I'll have to let my apartment go and move back home."

"Don't make any rush decisions tonight, Kayla."

"What other alternative do you see? There's the business, employees to deal with, and Mom's house—"

"Kayla. You don't have to go through this alone. Let me in. Let me help."

"With my mother?"

He leaned toward her and rested his elbows on his thighs. "You let me know what you need, and I'll do it."

Kayla smiled for the first time all night. "You're welcome to plan out the menus for next week, and I'll need another cook—"

"Funny."

"Why don't we go check out the cafeteria?" Kayla stared at her mom. "She's sleeping, and I could really use some coffee."

"And a shoulder to lean on?"

"Yeah. Especially that."

❧

Kayla chose a table in the back corner of the cafeteria, away from the group of nurses who chatted over cups of coffee. She stirred her own drink and watched the sugar slowly dissolve. The doctor's prognosis was still inconclusive. Possible surgery. . .inevitable extended physical therapy. . . This wasn't a simple take-two-aspirin-and-call-me-in-the-morning situation.

Ty slid into the chair across from her and slapped his hands against the table. "I convinced the chef to whip up a burger for you before he left for the night."

"You didn't." Kayla's stomach growled, reminding her that lunch had been hours ago and the piece of birthday cake hadn't been enough to take the edge off her appetite.

"Extra pickles, hold the mayo. Just the way you like it."

"Thank you."

"You're welcome." He leaned back, balancing his chair on two legs. "When my grandfather was sick, I had to learn that if I didn't take care of myself then I couldn't help him. Let me take you home after you're finished eating."

"Mom needs me here."

"Yes, she needs you, but Kayla, you have to realize she has a long road ahead of her. This isn't going to be over in a few days or even a few weeks. If you burn out from lack of sleep or not eating right, you won't be able to help her."

Kayla fiddled with the sugar wrapper in front of her, trying to calm her nerves. She'd never imagined how one moment in time could change her life so dramatically.

"Considering that tomorrow I'm going to have to turn in my notice for my apartment, talk to Jenny about working full-time, find out what kind of long-term care insurance my mom had—"

"I thought we just decided you can't do any of those things tonight."

"I know, but I have to do something. She's just lying up there, helpless." The reality of the situation hit her afresh, and tears began to flow down her cheeks. "I'm scared, Ty. I don't want to lose her this way."

"She has a good chance for a full recovery. The doctor said so."

"I am going to move into her house," Kayla said decisively. "She's going to need me once she comes home."

"I have to admit that makes sense. What can I do?"

"I need to find a mover."

"Consider it done." Ty held out his arm and flexed his muscles.

"Very funny." Kayla shot him a wry grin. "The house needs to have a few things done to get it ready for winter. Mom usually loves working outside, but that won't be possible for a while now."

He reached out and tucked a strand of her hair behind her ear. "It's going to be all right."

"Maybe. You never expect something like this to happen." She grasped his hand and pressed it against her cheek, wondering how she could have ever doubted him. "And there's one other thing. I'm sorry about all the things I said in the car. I can't blame you for my mom's unhealthy attitude toward men."

"Forget it."

"Kayla? Ty?"

Kayla turned to see the minister from their church, Randall Jenkins, walk into the cafeteria.

"I forgot to tell you I called the prayer chain at church," Ty told Kayla as the gray-haired man walked toward their table.

"I'm sorry I took so long to get here. I was in a meeting and just got your message." The older man pulled up a chair. "How is she?"

"She had a stroke and is paralyzed on her left side. It'll take a long time, but the doctor said a full recovery is possible."

The minister laid his hand on Kayla's shoulder. "I'm so sorry. What can I do?"

Kayla shrugged. "I don't know right now. She won't be home for a while. I'm only down here now because she's sleeping."

"I want you to know there are a lot of people at church who are willing to help. Once she's home, we can help provide meals and even someone to stay with her when needed."

Kayla felt the flow of tears begin again, overwhelmed by the show of love as the older man began to pray for complete healing for her mother as well as strength for her in the coming weeks.

Kayla looked up when he was finished. "Thank you."

He shoved his thick glasses up the bridge of his nose. "We're here for you. Call me if there's anything else that needs to be done."

"I appreciate it, too, Pastor Jenkins." Ty reached out to shake the minister's hand.

"Take my advice, Kayla. Go home and get some sleep."

Kayla yawned. "I will. Besides the fact that I'm out-numbered, I'm too tired to argue."

The waitress slid the plate of hamburger and french fries on the table in front of Kayla. Ty handed her the salt and pepper. "Then as soon as you're done eating, let's get you home."

nine

Kayla stifled a yawn and tried to concentrate on the fresh basil she was chopping. Between trying to keep the catering business going, packing up her apartment, and visiting her mother every day for the past two weeks at the hospital, she was exhausted. She yawned again then set down the sharp knife, forcing her eyes to focus. If she wasn't careful, she'd do something foolish and be the next one taken to the emergency room. And that was something she couldn't afford.

The back door squeaked open, and Jenny tottered through the entryway with two heavy sacks of fresh produce in her arms.

"You're early." Kayla smiled, wishing it was as easy to change her mood as it was to plaster on a happy face.

"Traffic was light. And besides, got to be prompt for the boss." Jenny flashed her a grin. "She can be an ogre at times."

"Very funny." Kayla couldn't help but chuckle at her friend's jovial expression. Jenny had been a lifesaver the past two weeks, not only in filling in where needed but also helping to keep Kayla's spirits up.

"How's your mom?" Jenny set the sacks on the counter then slid off her fleece jacket. With October halfway over, the lingering Indian summer that had kept temperatures pleasant was quickly fading into winter's cooler weather.

"She's making slow progress, but at least it's progress. I'm hoping she'll be home by the end of the week."

"That's good news, but I know all of this is hard on you."

Jenny squeezed Kayla's shoulder before hanging her coat on the rack behind the door. "I keep telling you to take some time off. You have enough qualified staff to fill in the holes, and I can run a tight ship. You don't have to do everything."

Kayla reached for the half dozen eggs she'd boiled earlier and began chopping them. An afternoon off was tempting, but one look at this week's schedule was enough to remind her they needed every person working full-time. "You know I appreciate the offer, but I'm the one Mom's counting on to ensure everything goes smoothly."

"An afternoon off won't bring about the demise of the company." Jenny started unpacking the produce, and while her motherly tone spoke volumes Kayla didn't miss the gleam in her eyes.

Kayla turned to Jenny and set her hands squarely on her hips. "What is it? You've got that I'm-dying-to-tell-you-something expression on your face."

"Who me?" Jenny laughed then held up her left hand. "Greg finally asked me to marry him last night."

"And you were going to tell me when?" Kayla squealed and grabbed her friend's hand, staring at the pear-shaped diamond. "It's stunning."

"I know. I never knew he had such good taste."

"He chose you, didn't he?" She gave her friend a hug. "When's the big day?"

"Sometime in the spring." Jenny went back to unloading the sacks. "What about you and Ty? You don't talk about him very much anymore. Isn't it about time for the two of you to follow us down the road toward marital bliss?"

Kayla frowned and dumped the basil and eggs in with the fresh crabmeat, wondering when Jenny had begun rooting for the man who once broke her heart. More times than she could remember she'd wanted to bare her heart to Jenny and Chloe, but something had always stopped her. Her mother's outburst at her birthday party had cinched her resolve to keep the details of their relationship to herself. This was just something she would have to handle on her own. Still, no matter what the rest of the world thought, Ty didn't need to prove himself to her. He'd already done that.

Kayla reached for a handful of scallions and started chopping again. "Knowing the way everyone feels about him, it's been easier just to keep our relationship private."

Jenny folded up the sacks and stuck them in a drawer. "You know we never meant for you to feel that way. The rest of us are just. . .cautious."

"Even after all this time? Surely even you can see he's changed, Jenny."

"Honestly, I'm starting to like the guy, but it doesn't matter what I think. You trust him, don't you? That's what counts."

The phone rang, and Kayla picked up the cordless receiver, thankful for the reprieve from Jenny's question. Of course she trusted Ty. It was everyone else who refused to give him a second chance. "Marceilo Catering."

There was silence on the line then those two haunting words again.

"He's guilty."

Kayla slammed down the phone.

"Wrong number?"

"Something like that."

A chill ran down Kayla's spine. She wasn't ready to connect the dots yet, but something wasn't right. Following the articles in the newspaper had continued to reveal that Abbott Financial Services was in serious trouble with the government, though no arrests had been made. A hundred and seventy-five million dollars couldn't have vanished without help. She'd known a year ago that Richard Abbott was grooming Ty for a position on the company's management team. He'd been next in line for chief financial officer and would have been the youngest ever to be appointed. Had Ty left the company in hopes of avoiding a bomb dropping, or had he truly been unaware of what was going on?

"Kayla."

She jerked her head up and caught Jenny's gaze. "Sorry."

"What's wrong?"

"Nothing. I'm just tired this morning." She'd tried hard to ignore any red flags, certain they were only her imagination working overtime. She had no idea who had been behind the phone calls she'd been receiving the past few days. And she hadn't told anyone. Not even Ty.

He's guilty.

The menacing words echoed though her mind, but she was still convinced even the old Ty wouldn't have stooped to defrauding the company. She'd never believe that. This was Ty. The man who loved her. Who visited her mom in the hospital. Arranged a group of guys from church to move her out of her apartment. Bought her tickets to the symphony. . . .

The blade of Kayla's knife stopped mid-stroke. "What's today?"

Jenny looked up from the schedule she was going over. "Thursday."

"No." Kayla waved her hands in front of her. "I mean, what is the date?"

"October twelfth."

"Oh no."

"What's the matter?"

Kayla set down the spoon she was using to blend the crab

mixture together and reached for her purse. Digging through the side pocket, she pulled out the red envelope. "This is what's the matter."

"What is it?"

"The tickets to the symphony. Ty gave them to me for my birthday."

"When is the concert?"

"Tonight. And I forgot."

"Uh oh."

"Uh oh is right."

"Tonight's the Bunners' anniversary party." Jenny left the clipboard on the desk and crossed the tiled floor. "I can handle it, Kayla. I might be a mathematician in disguise, but I can do this."

"Are you sure?"

"Haven't I been trying to get you to take some time off for days? This is perfect."

"Maybe you're right. Last night he insisted on taking me out to eat, and I almost fell asleep over dinner." Kayla leaned against the counter and mentally went over her schedule for the day. "I'll have time to go to the hospital this afternoon when the luncheon is over. That will still leave time for me to get ready for the symphony."

With renewed energy she sprinkled breadcrumbs over the crab mixture. Tonight wasn't a kink in her schedule; it was time with Ty. Something they both needed. Feelings of fatigue washed over her, but she ignored the impact. She could handle it.

If only she could ignore those two words.

❧

Ty knocked on Kayla's door at half past six. He'd heard the fatigue in her voice when he called her and had tried to convince her to stay in tonight. They could always go another night, but she had been insistent that she wanted to go. Not that a night out wouldn't be good for her, but she needed sleep more.

When she didn't answer, Ty knocked on the door again.

"Kayla?"

Digging into his pocket, Ty pulled out the key Kayla had given him in case of an emergency. This might not be technically classified as an emergency, but she should be home and wasn't answering. He was worried about her.

"Kayla," he said again, stepping into the apartment. Boxes lined the living room wall, ready for the people from church who were coming on Saturday to move her belongings to her mother's home.

"Kayla, it's Ty."

There was no answer. Ty glanced at his watch. Where could she be? She knew he was planning to pick her up for dinner.

Walking toward the couch, a wave of relief swept over him. Kayla lay curled up with a thick afghan covering her; she was sound asleep. Her cheeks were tinged with a hint of pink, and he resisted the urge to brush back a curl that had fallen across her forehead. Part of him still didn't believe he deserved her, but God had been gracious enough to grant him a second chance to win her heart.

All that stood between them now was Richard Abbott and her mother's approval. Visits to the hospital had already begun to bring out a softer side of Mrs. Marceilo, and Kayla never had to know the police had questioned him regarding the missing money. Or that they were still looking into his involvement with the missing funds. He'd find a way to avoid any backlash.

"Tell her."

Ty frowned at the insistent voice in the back of his mind. *"Tell her."*

The words came again, but he ignored them. He couldn't tell her. If he wanted her to trust him, telling her would only serve to drive a wedge between them. And that was something he couldn't afford. Ty tiptoed into the kitchen where he'd seen a pad of paper and pens and scratched out a note to let her know he'd come by. He'd been right when he'd tried to encourage her to skip tonight and go to bed early. She was exhausted. There would always be another night at the symphony.

Setting the note on the coffee table, Ty turned to leave.

"Ty?"

He stopped in the entryway. "Hey. You weren't supposed to wake up."

"What time is it?" Kayla sat up and rubbed her eyes.

"Six-thirty."

She rubbed her hand on her forehead. "I'm sorry. I must have fallen asleep."

Ty bent down to kiss her. "And that's exactly what you're going to do. I'm leaving, and I want you to get ready for bed."

"I can't, Ty. I've been looking forward to tonight." She struggled to get up, but he gently pushed her back onto the pillow.

"Kayla. You haven't even had time to think about tonight. All you need right now is to get some sleep. We'll do it again. I promise."

"But Jenny's covering for me at work and—"

"It's okay."

Kayla ran her fingers through her hair. "I'm sorry."

"For what?"

"For disappointing you."

"For disappointing me? You could never disappoint me."

Kayla's face broke into a smile. "I wish that was true. I've fallen asleep on you two nights in a row."

"I hope that isn't an indication of how boring I am."

"Don't worry. I can't imagine life with you ever being dull."

Ty leaned against the couch's armrest. "Just promise me that as soon as I leave you'll go to bed. These last couple of weeks have been hard on you, and you need to get your rest. Promise?"

"I promise."

"Then kiss me good night, and I'll leave."

"Tell her."

Ty ignored his conscience or God or whatever it was and instead reached over and kissed her again, wishing he didn't have to go. "I'll call you in the morning."

He walked out of the apartment, locking the door behind him. Surely God didn't expect him to tell Kayla everything that was going on. He'd risk losing what he'd worked to fix between them. No. That was a chance he simply wasn't willing to take.

❧

Kayla aimed the can of polish at her mother's dining room hutch and sprayed the lemony scented liquid onto the wood. Except for a few pieces of furniture still left to dust, she'd managed to do a thorough cleaning of her mother's entire house in one afternoon. Three weeks of trying to schedule her life around hospital visits and catering jobs had left her too exhausted to worry about the layer of grime accumulating in her mother's normally spotless house. Having her mother at home now added a new dimension to the situation, but at least she wouldn't have to make the daily trek to the hospital.

The loud crack of splintering wood sounded from outside.

Kayla turned to the large picture window overlooking the front lawn. Last time she'd looked, Ty had been raking the leaves in her mom's yard. What was he doing now?

An unmistakable thud followed. Kayla dropped the spray can on the hutch and ran to the front door.

Outside, Ty lay on his back beside a thick tree limb. Kayla's throat constricted. This couldn't be happening. Her mother lay inside barely able to function, and now Ty.

I can't handle anymore, Lord.

She ran across the yellow grass, the scene a blur from tears that threatened to escape. By the time she reached him, he was trying to sit up.

She stumbled over the limb. "You're okay?"

"I'm fine."

"What were you doing?" Kayla knelt beside him wanting to slug him for scaring her. "You might have broken something."

"Trust me. The only thing hurt right now is my pride." Ty stood to brush off a layer of dirt from the back of his jeans.

"You're sure you're not hurt?"

Ty walked around, as if to prove everything was in working order. "I'll have a few sore muscles, but certainly not anything to worry about."

"What were you doing up in the tree?" Kayla stood up to face him as a surge of anger coursed through her. He had no right to take chances and worry her this way.

"I was trimming a couple of those branches. Didn't want them to fall on the house. The second branch didn't fall, but I did." Ty rubbed his left elbow with his hand then stopped. "Why are you crying?"

She jutted out her chin. "I'm not crying."

"Then what is this?" He brushed away a tear from her cheek. "I'm okay, Kayla. Really."

She pressed her fists against her hips and fought the urge to lash out at him. "I'm not crying. I'm mad."

"Mad?" He pulled her toward him, but she pushed him away.

"Yes! Mad because you took a stupid risk and climbed my mother's tree. Mad because you fell out and scared me half to death. . .and mad because. . .because I can't lose you, too."

Silence hovered between them for a moment. Ty pulled her to him and hugged her. She could feel her heart pounding against his chest and hated the way she kept falling apart without any warning.

"You could have broken your neck or something." She looked up at him. "I can't handle anything else."

"Come here." Ty sat on the grass and pulled her down beside him. "You've been through a lot these past few weeks. Personally, I think you've done remarkably well."

She shook her head. "Remarkable because I'm having panic attacks every other day? This isn't me, Ty."

"Stop trying to be superwoman and let people help you." Ty grasped her hands and leaned forward. "And it's okay to cry."

Kayla frowned. Maybe he was right, but she was tired of crying and feeling as if she carried the weight of the world on her shoulders. She was tired of being tired. The doctors estimated a six-month recovery for her mother. If she couldn't make it three weeks without falling apart, how would she ever get through the coming months?

"I don't think I can do this, Ty. The home health nurses are great, but what about when that's over?"

"One day at a time is all you have to worry about." He tilted her chin up with his thumb.

"Didn't Jenny say she'd organize some women to help you clean?"

"Yes, but—"

"No buts. You should have asked for help. I'm here. Jenny and Chloe are willing to do anything for you. The church has offered to help. How does that verse about sharing one another's burdens go?"

Kayla cocked her head and shot him a smile. He was right. As always. The one person who could give her the push she needed to get going in the right direction again.

"What is it?" Ty asked.

"You should see yourself." She pulled a leaf from his hair.

"What?" He shook his head, and another leaf tumbled to the ground.

"You're a mess."

"And you're changing the subject."

Kayla jumped up and headed for a pile of leaves Ty had raked earlier in the day. She'd been cooped up inside long enough. What she needed right now was an old-fashioned leaf fight.

"Don't you touch that pile." He reached for her arm, but she was quicker than he was. "I'm not cleaning up this yard again."

"Oh, really?"

Kayla scooped up an armful of the crisp leaves, and as soon as Ty was close enough she threw them at him.

"Two can play this game, you know." Ty gathered up a pile. The leaves hit Kayla and fluttered to the ground as she scooped up another load and aimed for her target. Before she could let go, Ty ran toward her and tackled her, pinning her back to the ground.

"Give up?" Ty teased.

"Never." She blew a leaf off her face.

"Say uncle."

"Never!"

Kayla began to laugh as Ty reached for her sides and started tickling her. Squirming unexpectedly, Kayla slid out from under him and ran back to the tree.

"Are you giving up already?" Kayla poked her head out from behind the tree to watch him where he stood.

"No." His expression turned serious. "It's just good to see you laugh."

Kayla leaned against the rough bark. "Has it been that long?"

"Yes, it has." He walked toward her.

"You make me happy. That's why I couldn't stand it if something happened to you."

He gathered her into his arms and kissed her. "I always want to make you happy."

She felt a hot blush cross her cheeks. "We're in the middle of my mother's front yard."

"I'll stop." He kissed her one last time on the tip of her nose. "You're just hard to resist."

Kayla stepped back, looking at his tall, lean frame, and gave a prayer of thanks to God for bringing him back into her life. "I need to check on my mother, then finish cleaning the house."

"And I need to finish up here as well." Ty's cell phone beeped, and he grabbed it off the porch railing.

Kayla brushed off the front of her pants. "Who is it?"

Ty frowned and shoved the phone into his pocket. "It's nothing important. Just work."

"That was more than a my-boss-wants-me-to-work-overtime look."

"Everything's fine. Really." Ty grabbed the rake and eyed the scattered leaves. "And it looks as if I have just a few things to get done before dark."

❧

Ty waited until Kayla was back inside the house before pulling out his cell phone again. He'd almost broken down and told her the truth about the investigation, but the last thing she needed was another problem dumped on her.

He punched in Penny's number, thumping his foot against the ground until she answered. "Penny, it's Ty. What's going on?"

Silence filtered across the line for a moment until Penny spoke. "I thought you might want to know they found a stack of papers with your signature on them. And let's just say these weren't authorization forms to buy envelopes from a discount store."

"What are you talking about?" Ty combed his fingers through his hair and stared at the ground. "You know I'm clean, and I've given the government everything I have against Abbott—"

"I'm not sure that matters anymore. The government's fraud team isn't going away, Ty, and they're not stopping with Abbott."

Ty snapped his phone shut, wondering when the noose was going to tighten further and if there was anything he could do to stop it.

ten

"What about this one?" Jenny stood in front of a three-way mirror dressed in a satin wedding gown with embroidered flowers on the bodice. Tiny beads sewn into the skirt glistened in the soft light of the boutique.

Kayla reached down to spread out the ivory train then let it tumble to the ground in gentle waves behind Jenny. The Bee Gees played "How Deep Is Your Love" in the background, adding to the romantic ambience of the shop. Plymouth's Wedding Boutique had everything, including veils, hats, jewelry, and shoes, and was the perfect first stop for any bride-to-be.

Kayla folded her arms across her chest and eyed the gown. "It's beautiful, but so was the last one. And the one before that. . .and the one before that."

"That's the problem." Jenny laughed. "Just when I think I find something I like another one catches my eye."

Kayla chuckled at her friend's indecision. Choosing a wedding dress was proving to be more complicated than solving a complex mathematical equation. And they'd yet to look at flowers, music, and menus. At this rate six months wasn't going to be nearly enough time to plan the couple's wedding. Kayla had already decided they were going to have to take another afternoon off at some point and go into Boston where the selection catered more to Jenny's nontraditional tastes.

Kayla, on the other hand, loved the elegant feel of the shop.

Dresses with long trains, white gloves, and pearl-studded veils. . . . She took a step back and stared at her friend's silhouette in the mirror. A year ago she'd been the one standing on the low stool, modeling dress after dress for her own wedding. She'd chosen a matte satin gown with a sweetheart neckline and an A-line skirt that had formed a chapel train in the back. Returning it to the shop without ever wearing it had been enough to leave her in tears. But even that hadn't been as painful as finding out Ty wasn't the man she'd thought he was—or had wanted him to be. That revelation had ripped her heart in two.

She took in a deep breath and pushed away the memory. Things were different this time around. The thoughts gnawing at the back of her mind were nothing more than symptoms of her own insecurities.

"Kayla?"

Kayla glanced up at her friend. "Sorry. What did you say?"

"What about this one?" Jenny held up a lacy gown with dozens of white pearls sewn into the bodice.

Kayla pressed her lips together and tried to stay focused on Jenny. Today was her day, and she wasn't about to put a damper on it because of her own complicated love life. "I like it, though not as much as the one you're wearing."

"It's too simple, isn't it?"

"I didn't say that." Kayla eyed the dress. "It's only that the last one was too fancy, and the one before that didn't have enough lace."

"It's a bride's prerogative to change her mind." Jenny straightened the tiara atop her head and turned to the saleslady whose fixed smile implied she was used to fluttery brides who had no idea what they wanted. "Where's the one with the pale champagne organza fabric? I'd like to try it on again."

Kayla browsed through the racks while the saleslady went to look for the dress. "I loved the shimmering champagne-colored dress, but the diamond tiara has to go. Way too gaudy in my opinion."

Jenny studied her refection in the mirror then wrinkled her nose. "You're right."

Still waiting for the salesgirl to return, Kayla perused a nearby aisle before another dress caught her eye. "Look at this one."

Kayla ran her fingers across the satin material. The fitted bodice featured a U-shaped neckline and pearl accents. Roses and a trail of silver leaves ran down the skirt. If she was the one looking for a wedding dress, this one was close to perfect.

Except, of course, she wasn't looking.

"You should try it on."

Kayla's brow puckered at her friend. "I'm not engaged."

"You practically are."

"This is your day." Kayla studied the detail in the embroidered stitching across the bodice. It was completely different from the one she'd bought a year ago—but then she and Ty were completely different people today.

Jenny nudged Kayla with her elbow. "Try it on."

"Would you like to try that one as well?" The saleslady appeared behind them.

"No, but my friend would."

Before Kayla had a chance to argue, the two women steered her into the dressing room. Moments later she stood in front of the mirror, the bodice and slimming waistline fitting to perfection. Small pearls graced the sleeves as well as the bottom edges of the dress.

"It's breathtaking, isn't it?" Kayla could hardly believe her own reflection. Her cheeks were tinged pink, and she looked like a princess who'd just stepped out of the pages of a fairytale book. It took little imagination for her to picture Ty as her knight in shining armor coming to rescue her.

"Now you just have to get Ty to pop the question," Jenny said.

Reality smacked the air out of Kayla's lungs. She wanted him to ask her, but life had turned into a complicated muddle of confusion between caring for her mother and running her mom's business. Keeping up a relationship in the twenty-first century had nothing to do with castles and handsome knights. It had everything to do with honesty and trust.

"Our relationship isn't as simple as yours and Greg's."

"No relationship is simple." Jenny handed Kayla a gauzy veil with rhinestones and drop pearls surrounding the headpiece, then helped her slip it on.

It was a perfect fit for the dress. "If he does ask, will you be my bridesmaid?"

"You know I will." Jenny reached around the layers of satin to give Kayla a hug. "He makes you happy. I can't deny that."

He's guilty.

No! Kayla stared at her reflection in the mirror and tried to ignore the words that had continued to repeat over and over in her mind. "You're right. Ty does make me happy. Very happy."

If that were true, though, why did it sound as if she were trying to convince herself?

🌿

Ty rang the doorbell to Kayla's mother's house, then took a step back on the wide porch. Six months ago he never would have considered coming to Rosa Marceilo to talk about her daughter. She would have kicked him out in an instant. Today he stood at her front door, ready to wave the white flag if necessary. No matter what her stance, he was determined to do things right this time. And despite the obstacles that still seemed to stand in their way he wasn't prepared to put off their wedding any longer.

A home nurse opened the door then escorted him into the living room where Mrs. Marceilo sat in a recliner.

"Ty?" While her speech had improved tremendously with therapy, her left arm and leg still hung limp. "Kayla's not here right now. She—she's out with Jenny."

"I know." He shoved his hands into his back pockets. "I came to see you, actually. Do you have a minute?"

A crooked smile crossed her face. "I'm not going anywhere, and I. . .I can't get up to kick you out if that's what you're worried about."

The plump nurse stood in the doorway to the kitchen. "May I get the two of you some tea?"

Mrs. Marceilo nodded. "That would be nice, Hillary. Thank you."

Ty sat across from Kayla's mom on the faded blue couch, and it struck him how much Kayla had given up to move in with her mom. The country décor of the living room was a far cry from Kayla's more traditional tastes. She loved her dark mahogany furniture bought from local auctions, brightly colored wall murals, and shelves filled with books and photos. Most of the pieces she'd collected now sat in storage.

He fiddled with the edges of the embroidered pillow beside him. "How are you feeling?"

"My speech is improving, but I forget what I want to say. . . half the time. Physical therapy's a. . .nightmare, but they've tried to. . .convince me it's the only way I'll walk again." She grasped her limp arm, then let it fall onto her lap.

"Kayla told me they expect a full recovery."

"P–possibly. I suppose that depends on. . .on how hard I work." Mrs. Marceilo repositioned the afghan on her legs. "You. . .don't have to bore us both with a bunch of small t–talk, Ty. I've never hid the fact I. . .disliked you, and I'm b–betting you've felt the same way."

Ty stared at the framed quilt hanging on the wall behind Mrs. Marceilo's head and sent up a prayer for guidance. Apparently his regular visits to the hospital had done little to ease the strain of their relationship. Not that he'd expected to be received like the prodigal son, but something had to be done to ease the tension between them, for Kayla's sake, if nothing else.

The woman brushed a wisp of auburn hair from her forehead. Despite Kayla's heavy workload, he knew she managed to fix her mother's hair every morning, help her dress, and put on her makeup. It was a gift that had helped to build back the woman's confidence.

She pushed up her glasses and eyed him closely. "Even I have to admit. . .something's changed about you."

Her statement caught him off guard.

"Excuse me?" Ty leaned forward. He'd expected her to continue shooting barbs at him, not handing out hope for a truce.

"The Ty I knew wouldn't have made. . .daily visits to see some old woman unless it. . .unless it somehow fit into his agenda to get. . .what he wanted." Her expression softened slightly. "As hard as it is for me to admit. . .you've been there for my daughter."

Hillary brought in a tray with two cups of tea and a plate of cookies. She held the smaller drink in front of Mrs. Marceilo. "Can you handle this? It's hot."

"I'll be fine, thank you." Mrs. Marceilo took the cup with

her good hand and drew it to her lips.

Ty waited until the nurse had left the room before continuing. "I know I've made mistakes in the past, but I love your daughter, Mrs. Marceilo."

"And for whatever reason. . .she says you make her happy." Mrs. Marceilo set the tea down and reached for a chocolate chip cookie from the end table beside her. "These are my weakness."

Ty smiled and took one for himself. "Your daughter makes me happy, too. That's why I'm here."

"I had a feeling this. . .this visit didn't have anything to do with me."

He cleared his throat, wondering if the momentary truce would last once he stated his real reason for coming. "I want to ask Kayla to marry me, and I would like your permission."

A frown appeared on her face, deepened by the droop on her left side. "I don't recall you taking the time to ask my—my permission the last time you asked her."

Ty tried to ignore her disapproving gaze, wondering if she enjoyed making him squirm. Christ might have forgiven all his past mistakes, but that didn't always take away the sting of guilt. Or the burden others placed on him. "There are a lot of things I regret in my past. I want to do it right this time."

Mrs. Marceilo took another long sip of tea before saying anything. "Three months ago I—I would have thrown you out of the house at this point."

He noted the slight gleam in her eye. There was no doubt about it. She was enjoying herself.

Ty relaxed a bit. Two could play the game as well as one. "And today?"

"Somehow you've managed to convince me. . .you care about my daughter. And not only. . .her, I might add, but her decrepit mother as well."

"I beg to differ with that description."

"Always the diplomat, aren't you?" Mrs. Marceilo laughed, but a warning flashed in her eyes. "Don't ever walk out on her, Ty Lawrence, because if you do, I–I'll come after you. I won't have my daughter set up like a. . .like a trophy on some mantel. . .then forgotten. Do you understand me?"

"Yes, ma'am." While he intended to keep his promise, he also took her warning seriously.

"You'd better." Her hand began to shake, and she set the cup down. "I have to admit. . .I don't understand the changes."

"Or believe them?"

"Not completely."

Ty rubbed his jaw and prayed for an answer. "Christ, and the sacrifice He made, changed everything for me."

"That is what Kayla keeps trying to tell me." Mrs. Marceilo shook her head. "I used to believe. . .God cared about me. Then my husband left. . .me alone with a seven-year-old daughter and a trail of grief."

"I spent a lot of time blaming God for man's mistakes. Or more often than not, for my mistakes. He does care, Mrs. Marceilo. And so do I."

Tears pooled in her eyes, but she remained silent.

Ty leaned forward to rest his elbows on his thighs. "I'm not one to make promises lightly, Mrs. Marceilo, but I do have one—no, two—that I want you to hear. I promise to take care of your daughter and always put her first. And I also promise to take care of you."

Mrs. Marceilo blinked away the tears. "I never planned to like you. . .let alone allow you to marry my daughter."

And for the first time in a long time, Mrs. Marceilo smiled at him.

Two hours later Ty sat across from Kayla at the small table in the back of the restaurant, wishing he'd chosen a more creative way to propose than over dinner. The soft music and candlelight were nice, but nice couldn't compete with the first time he asked her to marry him. Sailing around Nantucket Island with caviar and a hired musician wasn't easy to compete with.

Ty squeezed the lemon into his water, then took a sip. "I visited your mother today."

"I really appreciate the effort you've made with her." Her smile confirmed the fact that swallowing his pride and talking to her mother had been worth it.

"A box of chocolate truffles now and then goes a long way."

"I'll settle for prawns and shrimp tonight. The menu looks divine."

A pony-tailed waitress approached their table. "Are you ready to order?"

Kayla told the waitress what she wanted, then scooted her chair back from the table. "I'm going to run to the restroom and wash my hands before they bring out the appetizers if you don't mind."

"Of course." Ty felt for the small velvet box in his sport coat pocket as she walked away and thanked God for second chances.

Kayla pushed her way through the crowded bar, wondering why they couldn't place the restrooms in a more convenient location for those in the restaurant. The lobby was filled with people waiting to be seated. Four years of waitressing in college made her sympathetic toward the employees who'd go home after closing with sore feet and aching backs. Not that she didn't still get her fair share of aches and pains after being on her feet all night for a catered event, but it still had to be easier.

Past the bar was a narrow hallway. A woman wearing a black dress and high heels stopped in front of Kayla, blocking her way.

Kayla tried to move past. "Excuse me."

The woman shoved a lock of thick, dark hair from her shoulder but didn't move out of the way. "I hope you enjoy the prawns."

Kayla shook her head. "I'm sorry."

"The chef was guilty of overcooking mine, but you're a bit of a chef yourself, aren't you? You understand the challenges of preparing that perfect meal. Especially for such a large crowd."

Kayla reached up to rub her temple. Her head was beginning to pound from the loud music coming from the bar. "Do I know you?"

"No. But I know a lot about you, and I have a message for your boyfriend."

"You must have the wrong person."

"I don't think so. Tell Ty to watch his back."

The woman brushed past Kayla, knocking her into the wall. By the time she regained her balance, the woman was lost in the lobby crowd. Apprehension swelled through Kayla's chest. It was time for her to stop pretending everything was all right in her relationship with Ty. That he hadn't been involved in something at Abbott Financial Services.

Fear rose in her throat as she hurried into the bathroom and locked the door behind her. Stepping up to the sink, she stared at her reflection. Her eyes had dark shadows beneath them from lack of sleep. Her cheeks were flushed, but she wasn't sure if it was from the warmth of the restaurant or the encounter in the hallway.

She pressed her hands against her chest. Her heart was racing so hard it pounded in her ears. She glanced at her left hand and rubbed the empty space on her finger. She'd hoped Ty was going to ask her to marry him tonight. Her mother had been vague about his visit, but what other reason would he have had to come out to the house to see her mom?

Someone tried the handle, then knocked on the door. Kayla jumped. If it was that woman again. . .

"Is someone in there?"

"I'm coming." Kayla splashed water on her face and quickly dabbed it with a paper towel.

The room blurred before her as Kayla walked back to the table. She slipped back into her chair, then pushed the plate of appetizers the waitress had brought while she was gone toward the middle of the table.

Ty reached out to take her hand, but she pulled away. "What's wrong? You look as if you've been crying."

"I need to get out of here." She grabbed her purse from the chair and slung it across her shoulder. "You and I need to talk."

eleven

Ty slammed the car door, then shoved the keys into the ignition in order to start the heater. He still had no idea what he and Kayla were doing sitting in the parking lot of the restaurant—without having eaten dinner—the night he'd planned to ask her to marry him. Somewhere, between ordering shrimp and washing up in the restroom, she'd shoved their entire relationship to the edge of a cliff and left it dangling without any explanation.

He'd planned for tonight to end with her saying yes to his proposal. Instead he looked at her rigid figure beside him. Jaw clenched, lips pressed together, hands clamped tightly. . . The only other time he remembered her being this irate was the night she called off their engagement. Acid churned in his stomach as he gripped the steering wheel. That wasn't going to happen again. He wouldn't let it.

He popped the peppermint he'd grabbed on the way out of the restaurant into his mouth, then fiddled with the plastic wrapper. "What's going on, Kayla?"

She folded her arms across her chest, still staring straight ahead. "Why didn't you tell me the government is investigating you in connection with Abbott Financial Services?"

Her words struck like a sledgehammer against his chest, and he fought to catch his breath. "I—I didn't tell you because I didn't think it mattered. I'm innocent."

The moment the words were out, he realized he'd said the wrong thing. Negating the situation also negated the importance of her in his life and his need for her. But that wasn't true. All he'd ever wanted to do was protect her, to protect their relationship.

He cleared his throat and hunted for an explanation that would make sense. "I—"

"You didn't think it mattered?" Her voice rose a notch. "Of course it matters. How can we have a relationship based on trust when you won't talk to me about things that affect your life?"

"Kayla, I'm sorry. I didn't want to drag you into it."

"No." She turned to him, her eyes flashing with anger beneath the white light of a street lamp. "You didn't think I'd let you back into my life with a possible indictment hanging over you."

Her words pinned him against the wall and condemned him in one fatal swoop. But there was more involved. Hadn't he wanted to protect her? "It's complicated, Kayla."

"I don't care how complicated things are. You should've told me."

He drew in a ragged breath. Trying to protect her was nothing more than an excuse. He'd ignored the Spirit's nudging to tell her the truth, and now he was paying for his own foolishness. "You're right. I was afraid I'd lose you. I didn't want you to think I'd been involved in anything illegal, to give you any reason not to trust me."

"Well, guess what? That's exactly what you did. And it's about to get even worse." The rosy flush in her cheeks was gone, replaced by a white pallor. "I've been getting phone calls."

Ty shook his head. "What do you mean?"

"Someone's been calling me, presumably to convince me you're guilty, and then tonight—"

"Whoa, slow down, Kayla. You never told me any of this."

"The same way you didn't tell me? Just remember I wasn't the one trying to hide something from you. I was hoping the phone calls were nothing but pranks or the wrong number. Tonight all the dots finally connected." She grasped the door handle as if wanting to escape. "I thought our relationship had changed this time, Ty. You told me honesty and trust were the keys to making this relationship work. . .but you lied to me."

"Wait a minute." He wanted to reach out to grasp her hand, but he stopped himself. "I never lied to you."

Her brow furrowed into a narrow line. "You never lied? The police interviewed you, didn't they?"

"They interviewed all the employees who worked for Abbott during the past five years. It's procedure."

"And the night you told me you were working late?"

He closed his eyes and tried to remember the details of that day. There had been a family emergency with one of the employees, and his boss had asked him to oversee the end of the month accounting. In the middle of updating the computer, the police had called. He'd spent an hour being grilled on everything from his job description to Abbott's lunch habits. It hadn't been an experience he'd like to repeat. But he hadn't lied to her. He just hadn't told her.

"I was working late that night. The police called me in about seven. I might not have told you about the interview, but I never lied to you."

"Tell me, Ty. Does the president of Farrington Cranberry Company know the last employee he hired to oversee his financial status might be indicted for fraud?"

"That's not fair, Kayla—"

"Isn't it?" Every ounce of trust he'd gained back from her

during the past couple of months vanished into the cold night air. "I don't know, but when I hire a person I like to make sure there's no chance they might spend the next thirty years in prison."

His stomach knotted at the statement. Losing his current job had been an issue he'd chosen to keep shelved in the back of his mind. No doubt the only reason he hadn't had to hit the unemployment lines was because his new boss was an old friend from college who knew that while his personal life might have been marred with a few imperfections, his professional ethics were spotless.

Right now, though, his concern had to focus on Kayla. "Tell me what happened tonight."

She blew out a hard breath. "A woman stopped me at the restaurant and wanted me to give you a message. She said you needed to watch your back."

"Who was she?"

"How should I know? Some woman in a black dress, who wasn't there to be my new best friend—I can tell you that much."

"I don't understand." Ty pounded his hands against the steering wheel.

Abbott.

The noose was tightening, and this was a message. A message that they were watching and could get to him—and Kayla. Ty felt his forehead bead with sweat despite the cold weather. It had been foolish to believe all of this would go away without Kayla's finding out. Foolish to think he could hand over convicting files without Abbott's turning against him. Foolish not to have listened to the Spirit's urging to tell her the truth from the beginning.

A trickle of fear seeped through him, growing each moment

as he tried to digest the implications. How low would Abbott stoop to ensure he wasn't implicated? The police had questioned Ty regarding the papers with his signature, and he thought he'd convinced them they'd been forged. The pieces were starting to come together. Was it all simply a warning to be quiet or part of a setup Abbott was putting together with the help of his lawyers? Ty had believed that cooperating with the police was all he needed to do, but now with Kayla involved. . .

He turned up the heater a notch as the outside temperature continued to drop. "Tell me more about the phone calls."

"Someone apparently thinks you're guilty, and for whatever reason they want me to know."

He hated the edge of bitterness her voice held. God had given them both a second chance, and for him to have blown it was almost more than he could handle. "I should have told you, and now. . ."

"And now what?"

"I need you to believe I was never a part of anything illegal." He looked up at her, but she avoided his gaze. "I turned in documents to the police that I hoped would lead to implicating Abbott. But Abbott's going to do everything he can to make sure he's not the one who takes the fall."

Ty thought back on the past few weeks. The car that had followed him. Misplaced items at work and at home. He'd tried to chalk it up to coincidence, but now he knew that wasn't true. Abbott was looking for something. Warning him they could get to Kayla. And they would do anything to save their own skins. Leaving the company might have been the right decision, but it had put him at the top of Abbott's list.

She folded her arms across her chest. "I want you to take me home, Ty."

He looked up at her wondering what to do now. What he could say to make things right? "Don't do this, Kayla. We can work this out."

The hard lines that had marked her face earlier had softened into a look of sadness. What hurt him most of all was that he'd let her down. Why hadn't he trusted their relationship enough to tell her?

"I'm sorry, Ty, but it's too late this time."

❧

Ten minutes later Ty watched Kayla slip into her mother's house without a look back. He'd told her once that their relationship would make it as long as they were honest with each other. Pulling out of the driveway, he pushed on the accelerator and sped down the road, wondering how he could have neglected the very thing he'd assured her was most important.

He slammed his fists against the steering wheel. Trust was something one earned, a fact he knew all too well. Yet in the process of proving himself to her he'd managed to destroy everything he'd worked so hard to gain. And possibly lost Kayla in the process.

Something ran across the road, and he jammed his foot against the brake to miss it. The car skidded sideways, striking the edge of the sidewalk with a jolt. The seatbelt jerked against his chest as the car came to a stop.

For a full thirty seconds Ty didn't move. The quiet roar of the engine competed with the accusations filling his head.

"Lean on Me."

He barely heard the words through the muddle. The wind whipped across the windshield. A car honked in the distance. Even the pounding of his heart seemed to echo in his ears.

"Lean on Me."

He stared at the dashboard. This time the words filtered through the noise of the chaotic world around him. He'd worked so hard in the past year to make things right: with God, with Kayla. And he thought he'd succeeded until tonight. The words *lean on Me* echoed through the recesses of his mind. Maybe that was the problem. Everything had been about his getting things right. Had he forgotten to put God in the equation?

Pastor Jenkins had preached Sunday on how salvation was a gift of God's grace. Never something a man could earn on his own merits. The thought was sobering. He'd spent his whole life working to get ahead, and his efforts had gained him huge financial success and status. But success came with a cost, and the price tag had been too high. He'd lost Kayla in the process. Yet even after realizing he needed a Savior he'd continued to go at things his own way.

Choosing to follow Christ wasn't the end. For too many years he'd only listened to his own voice. He was going to have to make it a habit to stop and listen to the Spirit's prompting. Learning to be quiet and hear God's voice might have kept him from losing Kayla.

Ty held up his hands in defeat. *I need Your help, Lord. Help me to listen for Your voice.*

He pulled back onto the road again, fighting the strong urge to drive back to Kayla's. There were too many things left unsaid between them; too many things needing to be resolved.

"Lean on Me."

Slipping into the turn lane, he swung a right toward his apartment. He still had no clue what the future held, but for the first time in weeks he knew he didn't have to go through it alone.

Kayla thanked Hillary for staying late, then walked the older woman to the door. Locking it behind her, she slumped against the wall. The last couple of hours had played out like a bad movie. She'd been certain Ty's visit to her mother would end with a proposal tonight. . .then everything changed in an instant.

Turning off the lights, she walked down the hall to check on her mother who'd gone to bed early and was snoring softly in her room. Kayla stood in the doorway of the bedroom and smiled at the look of peace on her mother's face. Her left eye still drooped, and the road ahead wasn't going to be easy, but her mother would make it.

Kayla sat down on her bed, wishing a good night's sleep would erase the weeks of fatigue that were piling up. Picking up her Bible from the bedside table, she flipped open the pages. Between running the business and taking care of her mom she couldn't remember the last time she'd had a quiet time with God. Or how long she'd been trying to handle everything on her own. Somehow she'd let her spirit become a dried-up well in the middle of the desert.

I just can't do this anymore, Lord.

She opened to the first chapter of second Corinthians, a recent passage in one of Pastor Jenkins's sermons, and started reading. The apostle Paul had always been a superhero in her eyes. The list of things he endured for the sake of the gospel read like a *New York Times* bestselling thriller.

Pulling her legs up under her, she stopped at verse six. Paul wrote how suffering produced patient endurance. How could suffering produce patience? Kayla rubbed her temples with the tips of her fingers. She'd never been shipwrecked or left in prison or even gone without a meal. Her struggles were real, but in the scope of what many had to endure she wasn't sure they even counted as trials. On top of that, patient endurance read more like an oxymoron than a word of encouragement.

She reread verses three and four. " 'Praise be to the God and Father of our Lord Jesus Christ, the Father of compassion and the God of all comfort, who comforts us in all our troubles.' "

All our troubles. Her mom's stroke. Ty's betrayal. The load of running the business while caring for her mother.

She continued reading the chapter, stopping again at verse nine. " 'This happened that we might not rely on ourselves but on God.' "

The truth seared through to her heart like a hot iron. That was what was missing in her life. How long had she spent her time relying on her own efforts to take care of everything? She claimed to follow Christ but was all too quick to grab the steering wheel and head off in her own direction. Controlling the business. Controlling her mother's recovery. Controlling Ty.

Tears she'd held back for weeks poured down her cheeks like healing rain, and the love of her heavenly Father enveloped her. The future was still uncertain, but one thing wasn't anymore. This time she was going to put her trust in the One who created her.

ža

Ty parked his car in his spot, then locked the doors before heading up the sidewalk toward his apartment.

"Ty Lawrence?"

Ty stopped short of the small patio and turned around. "Yes?"

"My name's Samuel Lance. I'm a law enforcement officer for the State of Massachusetts." The man flashed a badge beneath the bright street lamp as he took a step toward him. "You're under arrest for accounting fraud and other illegal activities in connection with our recent investigation into Abbott Financial Services."

twelve

Kayla combed out a section of her mom's hair, then clamped it into the curling iron, wishing she could spend the rest of the morning in bed. She'd finally fallen asleep around one, but her dreams had been filled with Ty. Already she missed him, torn between her heart's longings and the common sense that constantly reminded her she needed to stay away from him. Even putting her trust back into God's hands had become a minute-by-minute effort.

"Are you almost done?"

Kayla's focus switched back to the task at hand. "One section left."

Her mom worked to fasten the top button of her blouse that had come undone. "You know you don't have to do my hair every morning, Kayla."

"I know I don't have to, but I want to." For once she was thankful for the distraction. Between her mom and the business, staying busy would make the pain of letting Ty go easier. Or at least she hoped it would.

Her mother's hand shook as she fought with the shirt.

Kayla reached down to help. "Let me do that—"

"No!"

Kayla drew back her hand and bit her lip as her mom continued to struggle. Her fingers fumbled with the buttonhole. It was all Kayla could do not to finish the chore herself. Finding the balance between helping her mother and letting her struggle to relearn simple tasks had proved to be difficult.

The stroke had added depression to the list of symptoms her mom had been forced to accept. All of which added up to a new dimension of tension between them.

Her mother jerked the button off and threw it onto the floor. For a few seconds neither of them moved.

"I'm sorry." Her mom let her good arm drop into her lap defeated.

"It's okay." Kayla moved the curling iron to the last section, deciding to leave the button on the floor for now.

"No, it's not." Her mom's leg shook. "Since when do I have to rely on—on my daughter and nurses to button my shirt?"

Tears pooled in her mother's eyes. Kayla set the curling iron down and wrapped her arms around her. Frustrations over her relationship with Ty seemed minimal compared to the life-changing challenges her mom faced.

Kayla bit back her own tears of empathy. "I remember when I was in third grade, and I wanted curls like Abigail Mentor's. You must have spent an hour fixing my hair every morning before school."

"And your curls were much prettier than Abigail's. . .weren't they?" Her mother's smile emphasized the droop on the left side of her face, but at least she seemed to have forgotten the button for now. "I wanted to see you last night. How was your dinner with Ty?"

With Ty on the top ten list of topics to avoid, Kayla hadn't expected the subject to come up and wasn't sure how to approach it. Another argument was the last thing she wanted. "I understand he came to visit you yesterday."

"He did. . .and we had a nice time. What happened at dinner?"

Kayla quirked an eyebrow at her friendly tone. "There's nothing to tell."

Her mom strained to look up at her. "Don't tell me the two of you. . .got in a fight?"

Kayla shook her head, confused. Even after her mom had agreed to keep her opinions of Ty to herself, nothing had really changed. The stroke had just postponed the inevitable explosion she was convinced was coming. Genuine interest in their lives wasn't what she'd expected.

Kayla began to comb the short curls into place. "Why the change of heart, Mom? You're acting as if you like him. But he's the bad guy, remember. The one who's stealing your daughter away, bound to break her heart."

"Not according to everything. . .I've ever heard from you." Her mom pointed to a gold-foil box on the bedside table. "You'd be amazed how far a box of chocolates goes when you've been living on hospital food."

"He said something about that." She still didn't get it. Since when did peace break out? "He was going to ask me to marry him, wasn't he?"

Her mom reached up to push a curl into place on the side of her head. "I'd say that's between you and Ty."

"Mom. I need to know."

"He came to ask my permission to marry you."

"And you agreed?"

Her mom nodded slowly. "Lying in a hospital bed for almost three weeks makes. . .you look at things differently. He's good to you. And as much as I haven't wanted to admit it, he's been. . .good to me as well."

Kayla sprayed some hairspray to set her mom's hair in place, making a mental note to schedule an appointment with the hairdresser for a perm. Her mom did have a point. Making sure the outside of her mother's house was ready for winter was only one of the things he'd done to help ease

Kayla's load. He'd fixed the garbage disposal, insulated the windows, changed the smoke detector batteries, and the list went on and on.

Her mom slid on her glasses. "He also mentioned how easy it is to blame God for our mistakes. I can't say. . .I've ever really thought about it that way."

Kayla squeezed her eyes shut for a moment and sent up a prayer for wisdom. If she was going to rely on God for His wisdom and help in her life, now was as good a time as any to start. If her mother was opening her heart to God, what she needed to tell her about Ty was going to make things worse. How many people had been turned off from God and consequently church because of the behavior of the very people sitting inside?

"There are some things you need to know about Ty, Mom."

Kayla sat down on the edge of the bed beside her mom and told her everything. From Ty's involvement in the government's investigation into Abbott Financial Services, to the strange phone calls, to the woman at the restaurant. The emotional weight she'd carried home the night before had shifted from anger to sadness. Maybe reality would hit her at some point. Right now she still felt numb.

"I'm so sorry you've had to go through this." Her mom reached out and grasped Kayla's fingers. "And I know this is going to sound. . .crazy coming from me, but I think you need to consider the fact that Ty's innocent."

Her brow pinched together. Those were the last words she'd expected to hear from her mom. "Whether or not he's innocent isn't really the point. He kept the truth from me. That's not a relationship to base a healthy marriage on. And it goes back to the same problems we dealt with a year ago. It's a matter of trust."

"What if he was simply trying to protect you?"

Kayla shook her head. She couldn't believe what she was hearing. Unplugging the curling iron, she marched across the room and opened the heavy, mauve drapes. Outside, dark storm clouds reflected her mood. Why was her mother defending Ty? A box of chocolates wasn't nearly enough incentive to blind a person to the truth of the situation.

Her mom struggled to add blush to her cheeks. "I'm serious, Kayla. Even after everything you've told me. . . something's not right."

"It seems pretty straightforward to me." She folded her arms across her chest, resisting the urge to take the makeup brush away from her mom to finish the job herself. "The bottom line is, whether or not he was involved, the fact remains that he didn't trust me enough to tell me what was going on. How could he hide the fact that he's one of the government's suspects? It doesn't get much bigger than that."

"I've kept things from you throughout the years to protect you."

"I'm not a child anymore, Mom. I don't need to be protected."

The doorbell rang, and Kayla fled from the room, grateful for the interruption. Since when did her mother defend Ty and his underhanded actions? If anything, her mom should be on her side; but instead it was as if she'd fallen into Alice in Wonderland's rabbit hole and ended up in the twilight zone.

The doorbell chimed again. Kayla glanced at her watch as she hurried through the living room. Eight in the morning was too early to expect company, and Hillary wasn't coming for another hour.

Kayla paused at the door. If it was Ty, she didn't want to see him. She might have realized she couldn't do things without her heavenly Father's help, but that didn't mean she was ready to deal with the emotional tsunami Ty was certain to evoke.

Leaning forward, Kayla glanced through the peephole, then let out a sigh of relief. Chloe stood on the porch, dressed in a red jacket, with a matching knit hat and gloves.

Kayla unlocked the door and flung it open. "Hey, this is a nice surprise."

Chloe stepped out of the cold and into the warm entryway before giving Kayla a hug. "Honey, I need to talk to you about something."

"And how are you this morning? You always were one to get straight to the point." Kayla caught Chloe's frown, and a shot of adrenaline flashed through her. "What's wrong, Chloe? Is it Nick or Jenny? Or the boys?"

Chloe stood in the entryway and pulled off her gloves. "No, sweetie. I hate to be the bearer of bad news, but it's about Ty."

"What's wrong, Chloe?"

"He called Nick last night a little after nine."

Kayla's head began to spin. Ty had left her place around seven, and she assumed he'd gone home. If he'd been in an accident, or even worse—what if Abbott had done something to him? "What happened? Is he hurt?"

"No, honey. Ty's been arrested."

Kayla felt her knees give out as Chloe helped her to the couch. Surely she hadn't heard her friend correctly. The company might be under investigation, but that didn't mean Ty had been a part of the corruption.

He's guilty.

She dismissed the condemning words that had haunted her the past few weeks. Ty couldn't be guilty. Sure, she'd been furious with him for not telling her the truth. For not trusting her to be able to handle what was happening in his life. But she'd never believe he could have been involved in something criminal.

She rubbed the back of her neck and stared at a spot on the carpet. When was the last time she'd had the carpets cleaned? She'd need to call and have someone come out—

"Kayla. Are you all right?"

"No." She shook her head and tried to erase the distractions as she looked up. "This can't be happening, Chloe. I don't understand."

Chloe sat across from her and took her hands. "Ty's worried about you. He insisted I come to your house and tell you in person. He didn't want you to find out on the phone or worse on the news."

Kayla glanced at the television that sat in the corner of the living room. Abbott Financial Services was no mom-and-pop business. They'd made the Fortune 500 list the past three years in a row. Ty's face would be plastered across TV screens and newspapers from Boston to San Francisco. The very thing he'd hoped to avoid.

"What's he been charged with?"

"Securities fraud and inflating stock prices. He was picked up last night by the Securities and Exchange Commission that's working with local law enforcement."

"What about Richard Abbott?"

"He could always be next. But, according to the prosecuting attorney, the evidence doesn't point to him."

"I don't believe it." Kayla pinched the bridge of her nose with her forefingers, refusing to cry. "This is serious, isn't it?"

"Very."

"And what if he's guilty?" Kayla's voice caught in her throat.

Chloe squeezed her hands. "I know none of us has been very supportive of your relationship with Ty, but that doesn't mean I think he could be guilty of defrauding a company of millions of dollars. All you can do right now is take things one day at a time and pray. Nick's a good lawyer and will do everything he can to get him off."

Put your trust in Him, Kayla. That's all you can do.

Kayla tried to steady her breathing, repeating the words over and over in her mind. "Is Nick there with him?"

"He's working to get him out on bail, but that's going to be tough. He promised to call me as soon as he finds out anything."

Kayla walked to the window. She thought her world had fallen apart last night when Ty admitted he was under investigation, but she'd never believe he was guilty of accounting fraud. Surely her instincts weren't that far off a second time.

"I have to do something." She stared out across the yellow lawn trying to work her mind around both Ty's arrest and what she needed to do about it. "I'll call Jenny and ask her to cover for me today."

Chloe got up and stood beside her. "What are you talking about?"

"Penny was Ty's secretary in Boston, and she worked for him for years. She has to know something."

"I'm sure the police have already questioned her, Kayla."

"I know, but they might have missed something, and I have to know the truth about him this time." Everything suddenly became clear. Maybe it was crazy, but there was no way she could stay here and wait for something to happen. Penny would have access to inside information that might prove Ty's innocence. "I'm going to Boston."

❧

Kayla shifted her umbrella to block the downpour as she ran toward the Abbott Financial building. Shivering beneath her long black coat, she wondered for the umpteenth time if her impulsive decision had been a mistake. She hadn't even taken the time to try to call Ty after Chloe's bombshell announcement. If the authorities would even let her talk to him.

She shivered again, but this time it wasn't from the cold. She needed answers before she could face him. Going to his old place of work had seemed to be the first logical step. Or at least it had seemed logical at the moment Chloe told her Ty had been arrested and Nick had just been brought in as his criminal lawyer. She was no Sherlock Holmes, but she was on the verge of another broken heart and had to do something. Besides, no matter how jumbled her personal feelings were at the moment toward Ty, she wasn't going to walk away this time without finding out the entire truth.

The four-story building rose before Kayla. Standing on the edge of the sidewalk beneath the outside awning, she stared up at Abbott Financial Services before taking a deep breath and heading inside. Her mother's insistence on Ty's innocence had surprised her—and convicted her. What if he was innocent and had only meant to protect her?

She crossed the lobby's polished tile floor, knowing that for now she owed him the benefit of the doubt. His methods of trying to protect her could be discussed at another time.

Five minutes later the elevator stopped on the third floor, and the doors opened to reveal the large reception area. It had been over a year and a half since Kayla had walked into the plush Boston office. Nothing had changed, from the overstuffed gray couch and chairs to the rich purple and silver accents.

"May I help you?" A receptionist looked up from a computer screen and waited for her response.

Kayla's stomach lurched.

You can do this.

She cleared her throat and caught the young woman's gaze. "I have an appointment with Penny Waterford."

The receptionist glanced at the calendar in front of her, then raised her penciled brows. "You have an appointment with Miss Waterford? She's an executive assistant who doesn't normally talk to clients."

"I spoke to her this morning, and we're having lunch."

"O–kay." The woman picked up the phone, mumbled a few words and hung up. "She'll be out in just a minute. Take a seat over there."

Kayla had just sat down when Penny walked into the room. The woman had cut her blond hair into an attractive bob, but other than that the petite assistant looked the same as when Ty had first introduced them at a company Christmas party two years ago.

"Kayla, it's good to see you again." Penny held out her manicured hand in greeting. "I was surprised to hear from you and even more surprised when you said you wanted to meet me here in person."

"I appreciate your taking the time to see me. Is there somewhere we could talk in private?" She wasn't in the mood for small talk and formalities.

"There's a bistro down the street." Penny slid a black coat on over her stylish purple skirt and blouse. "It's close enough to walk to and stays pretty quiet during lunch."

"That's fine."

Fifteen minutes later they were seated at a corner table with bottles of sparkling water. Aromas of garlic and onions coming from the kitchen did little to whet her appetite, and she wasn't sure if she'd be able to eat the chicken salad she'd just ordered.

"I was so upset when I heard about Ty's arrest this morning." Penny took a sip of her drink, seemingly relaxed despite the heavy atmosphere that must pervade the office after yesterday's arrests. "He was always a good boss. He worked hard and treated me well."

Kayla poured her flavored water into a glass full of ice. "Who do you work for now?"

"The big CEO himself. Richard Abbott."

"Wow! That must have been a nice promotion."

Penny set down her drink and nodded. "His secretary went on maternity leave then quit, and let me tell you, the extra income that comes with working for the CEO of the company can't be beat. Unless you count the recent government investigation."

"I'll get straight to the point, Penny. You knew Ty better than anyone I can think of here in Boston. Have you been in contact with him since he left?"

"Sure. He's called me several times over the past few months. We all knew the government was asking questions, and he seemed interested to know what exactly was going on. I always assumed it would disappear. I never thought anyone I knew, especially Ty, could actually be guilty."

Kayla leaned forward in her chair. "You don't think he did it, do you?"

"I—I don't know, Kayla." Penny's friendly smile faded. "I hate to burst your bubble, but as much as I liked Ty I think the authorities have the right man this time."

The dozen or so tables around them blurred from view as the walls closed in around her. The instrumental music in the background churned in her head like fingernails on a chalkboard. Voices slurred together into a muddled roar.

Kayla tried not to panic. "What are you saying, Penny?"

"They think he tried to clear most of the damaging stuff from his computer, but they were still able to find enough evidence to obtain an arrest warrant. Apparently he also handed over some documents to the police implicating Richard Abbott, but from what I heard most of those documents were well-thought-out forgeries."

"What?" Kayla shook her head. Ty might be brilliant when it came to numbers, but forgeries? It didn't make sense.

"I'm sorry." Penny took another sip of her water. "I know you didn't come here to hear me confirm what the police are saying, and I wish I didn't have to, but as Abbott's own protégé Ty was next in line for the job of chief financial officer. He had access to files and data that few other people in the entire company had."

Kayla knew she was grasping at straws, but she wasn't ready to stop yet. "Do they think he was the only one involved?"

"The authorities are looking at two other top managers. I knew them both. It's been a tremendous blow to the company, though we're all hoping we can put the scandal behind us as soon as possible in order to move forward."

"I guess I thought this had to have all been a big mistake. I mean, Ty and I have had our differences, but he's not a criminal." Kayla's temples began to pound. Something wasn't right, but she had no idea what. "Had you ever noticed anything out of the ordinary when you worked with him?"

Penny fiddled with the paper napkin between her fingers. "I debated whether or not I should pass this on to you, and I'm still not sure—"

"I have to know the truth."

"I had noticed some discrepancies for the past year or so and decided to start keeping copies of files." Penny pulled a flash drive from her purse and set it on the table. "I handed this over to the police three days ago, keeping copies for myself. I never told Ty what I was doing. I guess because I didn't believe he might be guilty. But all that's changed now, Kayla. I'm afraid the police have the right man. As far as I'm concerned, Ty's guilty."

thirteen

Kayla clicked on the small, fringed lamp in her mother's living room, then fell back against the couch cushions. The hour-and-a-half drive home from Boston to Farrington hadn't been enough time to erase the shock of Penny's convicting words. Instead it had resurrected all the old feelings of mistrust Kayla had managed to store away in the back of her mind these past few months. And brought with it a finality she hated. Ty was guilty, and there was nothing she could do to change that.

She rubbed the back of her shoulder with her fingertips to loosen the heavy knots in her muscles. Having Ty back in her life had been like the answer to an unspoken prayer. She'd never loved anyone the way she loved him. Even talking with him last night hadn't completely taken that away. But now everything had changed.

She'd tried to find a hole in Penny's story, anything that would prove Ty's innocence. But Ty's former secretary had no reason to lie to her. Penny's heart wasn't involved, allowing her to see the truth for what it was. Something Kayla had been unable—or perhaps unwilling—to do. Failing to see the truth at this point would do nothing but bring her even more heartache in the future. Just like telling him good-bye might not be something she got over quickly, but it was what she had to do.

She picked up the cordless phone off the end table and dialed his home number, realizing her mother had been right all along. People didn't change. Not really anyway. Ty was no different from the man he'd been the day she broke off their engagement. Whether or not he was guilty was no longer in the equation. He'd purposely kept too many things from her. And she couldn't pretend any longer that it was all right.

The phone rang a half dozen times, then switched to the answering machine.

She took a deep breath to steady her nerves. "Ty, this is Kayla."

She squeezed her eyes shut, wishing all this would go away. But the words *he's guilty* wouldn't let her forget.

Her hands shook as she held the phone against her ear. "Listen. I know you're in good hands with Nick, and I'm sorry for all that's happened, but I can't do this any longer. Please don't call me or try to contact me. I'm sorry...."

Kayla hung up the phone, not knowing what else to say. Maybe because there simply wasn't anything left to say. She'd taken a chance and given away her heart, quite certain now that she'd never get it back.

❧

The next morning Kayla piped the last layer of crimson frosting on the three-tiered wedding cake, then stood back for a final inspection. The Walker/James wedding had quickly become the wedding of the year in the small town of Farrington. Two families in the cranberry business who'd lived in the area for generations were finally tying the knot, and the fact that Marceilo Catering had been chosen to do the wedding was an extra bonus for the small company.

Kayla had decided to finish the cake at the church, which was now in the final stages of preparation for the seven o'clock ceremony. Jenny was on her way in the van with the majority of the food they would be serving from the newly refurbished kitchen; it was in the building's east wing where the full dinner reception would be held. Round tables with lacy white covers had been set up, along with yards of white and ruby red tulle, elaborate rose petal centerpieces, candles, and twinkling white lights.

She should be pleased with her staff's efforts, but instead the wedding only served to remind her of everything she'd lost. She'd seen clips on the news last night of how Ty had been released on bail until the upcoming trial. Chloe had told her that, despite his continued stance that he was innocent, he'd also lost his job with Farrington Cranberry Company.

She set the empty bowl of frosting in the sink and turned on the hot water. A part of her felt guilty for not being there for him. He'd stayed beside her every step of the way of her mother's recovery, from visiting her in the hospital to helping out at the house. Wasn't that enough to prove the man had changed?

The door banged open against the inside wall as Jenny entered the kitchen with her hands full of boxes of appetizers. "Kayla, we have a problem."

Thoughts of Ty vanished for the moment. There was a job to do, and it was up to her to run things in a professional manner. "What's wrong?"

Jenny set the containers on the counter and frowned. "One of our suppliers called ten minutes ago. He can't get the strawberries he's been promising me all week. Off season or not, the bride wants chocolate-covered strawberries."

"Then we'll give her something even better."

"What?"

Kayla rested her hands on her hips. "Is it too late to make those chocolate mousse dessert puffs we served last week? They were a huge hit and not too hard to make for an up-and-coming caterer like you."

Jenny grinned as she glanced at her watch. "I can have them ready by four, which should give us plenty of time."

"Good. I'll help you unload the van, then finish setting up here while you take care of the mousse. What about the other staff?"

"They'll be back here in a couple of hours with the rest of the food. Everything's on schedule."

"Great." Kayla headed for the van.

"Wait a minute, Kayla." Jenny started to follow then stopped. "Are you okay about all of this? I mean a wedding probably isn't on your top ten list of jobs you'd like to take right now with all that's happened in the past twenty-four hours."

Kayla shrugged, wishing her friend hadn't brought up the subject. "I can't exactly turn away business because I can't win at romance."

"I saw him on the news last night."

"So did half the state of Massachusetts." Kayla hurried out the back door and shivered at a gust of wind. Tonight's predicted snowfall would either add a romantic touch to the wedding or cause havoc in getting the guests here. She was fervently praying for the former.

Jenny hurried outside behind her. "I think he's innocent."

Kayla braced her hands against the van door before popping it open. Why couldn't everyone just drop it? The last thing she needed right now was a distraction. And thinking about Ty was a distraction. He was out of her life, and nothing anyone said or did was going to change that. "How can you have spent the past few months believing I was making another mistake and now, when I finally see the truth, you decide the man is innocent? Don't do this to me, Jenny. I can't handle it."

"I expected you to believe him."

Kayla felt her blood pressure rise as she grabbed a large container of cut-up fruit. "What I think doesn't change the reality of what happened."

"What if he was set up?"

Kayla froze. "What are you talking about?"

"I was over at Chloe's last night. Nick's looking into this angle. There have been too many strange things happening. The phone calls you received, the woman at the restaurant, Ty being followed and his house gone through—"

"What? He never told me about that." Kayla swallowed her irritation. She piled another container on top and hurried back into the church.

"Just hear me out, Kayla." Jenny grabbed the groom's cake and followed on her heels. "Nick's theory is that someone, namely Richard Abbott, is trying to scare Ty. He might not fight back if he knew they were watching him and could get to you."

Kayla spun around and planted her fists on her hips. "So what do you think I should do? Call him and tell him everything's okay?"

Jenny seemed to ignore the hint of sarcasm in her voice as she set the cake down on the counter. "I think you need to pray about it, but Ty was at Nick and Chloe's house last night as well, and in all honesty I think he's more upset about losing you than the upcoming trial. And you have to admit, no matter how professional you try to be, you're just as miserable. I don't know what'll happen, but my gut tells me there's more going on here than we can see from the surface. Ty might have been a workaholic in the past, and while it might have affected your relationship it's not a federal crime to be a jerk. Richard Abbott, on the other hand, apparently has a few skeletons in his closet that they're looking into. If the theory's true, I know even you wouldn't want Ty to take the fall for some rich man and his lawyers. And you certainly won't want him to go through this alone."

Kayla felt her lungs constrict, and she fought to breathe. What if he was innocent and she wasn't there for him?

Jenny moved in front of Kayla. "What does your heart say? Not your head or the facts. What does your heart say?"

"I don't know."

Kayla set the food down on the counter and clenched her fists at her sides. It wasn't fair. How had things gotten so complicated? She needed some time to think. . .and pray. She caught Jenny's gaze. "I know we've still got a lot to do, but you're right. I need some time to pray. Thirty minutes. An hour tops."

Jenny smiled and nodded. "You got it."

❧

Kayla walked down the center aisle of the auditorium toward the prayer room, stopping on the thick carpet to finger a red satin bow that hung on the end of one of the pews. Those setting up for the wedding must have gone to lunch because the sanctuary was quiet now. A quiet that would be replaced this evening with the joyful presence of family and friends of the couple pledging to spend the rest of their lives together.

She made her way toward the prayer room, feeling a sense of despondency grow with every step. Sunlight filtered through the stained glass window above the front baptistery, casting a golden glow over the large brass archway decorated with white organza and roses. Candles graced the front pews adding to the romantic feel of the room.

Had it only been a few short weeks ago when she had tried on a satin gown in the shop with Jenny and dreamed of her own wedding day in this very church? She thought she'd been given a second chance for love with the man who'd captured her heart. All she had left now were the shredded remnants of her heart. . .and lost dreams of what they could have had together.

What do I do now, Lord?

There were no answers this time, only the steady pounding of her heart.

Her heart.

Words spoken to her by her mom and friends flooded through her mind. *What does your heart say, Kayla, not your head? . . . What if he's only trying to protect you? . . . He's stood by you during your mother's illness. . . . Ty's innocent. . . .*

Ty's innocent.

But was he? Kayla pressed her fingertips against her temple. Was God using her friends and family to show her the truth?

Kayla slipped into the prayer room and sat down on the empty wooden bench. "I don't know what to do, Lord. I don't know if I can go through the rejection again if I'm wrong."

She fought to clear her mind, searching for the words as she spoke aloud. "What if he is guilty? That means he's lied to me, and even if he is innocent he never told me the truth about what was happening. Trust will always be an issue between us."

Kayla drew a tissue from the box beside her and blew her nose, wondering if Nick's theory had any merit. Even if Ty was innocent, the case wasn't going to disappear tomorrow. Abbott must be desperate to end things. Stock prices for the company had already dropped significantly as shareholders awaited further news from the government's investigation. And in the meantime Abbott would have the financial backing to do whatever it might take to frame Ty.

She held her head in her hands. Sixteen months ago Ty's true character had come out—even when she didn't want to see it. But things were different this time. Hadn't Ty proved he wasn't the same man? That he'd truly decided to follow Christ?

Convicted, she picked up her cell phone to call Ty.

"Kayla?"

She turned to the door, but all she could see was a dark silhouette of a man. The figure lunged toward her and grabbed her arms. The cell phone flew out of her hand and slammed against the wall. She tried to scream, but instead a blistering pain shot through her head, then darkness.

fourteen

Ty sat on the edge of the twin bed and stared at the colorful wall decal of Winnie the Pooh. Nick and Chloe had been gracious enough to give him a quiet spot in Brandon's room where he could spend some time thinking and praying. The thought of sitting home alone had become anything but appealing.

He clasped his fingers around the edges of the mattress, still wondering when he'd wake up from this nightmare. Four months ago he'd walked out of the executive office suites of Abbott Financial Services, certain he'd be able to find a way to help convict the company's crooked CEO. Somewhere along the line the tides had shifted, and now he was the one with the Securities and Exchange Commission, along with a half dozen other entities, breathing down his neck

This wasn't the way things were supposed to play out.

I don't understand, God. I gave my life to You, and now I'm looking at the possibility of spending the next twenty years in prison for something I didn't do.

None of it made sense. Not that he'd ever believed becoming a Christian guaranteed a happily-ever-after life, but what happened to *ask and you will receive* or *come to me, all who are heavy burdened*? Between his relationship with Kayla, her mother's stroke, and the fallout from Abbott Financial, he'd worn out his knees spending time in prayer. And for the first time he was beginning to wonder to what avail.

Ty picked up a throw pillow from the bed and flung it

against the pale blue wall. Admittedly part of this whole mess was his fault. How much had he lost because of his decision to keep things from Kayla? In an attempt to shelter her from the truth he'd pushed her away, losing any trust that had been gained between them.

He glanced around the small room that looked like a scene straight out of Pooh Bear's Hundred-acre Wood and felt the heavy ache of loneliness. Losing his career and facing jail time were difficult enough to comprehend. Losing Kayla was even worse. He'd imagined them with children five years down the road: a boy and a girl, or maybe two of each. He really didn't care as long as they could be a family. That was all he'd ever wanted.

I don't understand, Lord.

He gazed at the Bible lying on the edge of the bed but didn't pick it up. He'd spent half the morning searching for a word of encouragement to hold on to. Some promise that offered relief in the light of losing everything. But nothing had spoken to him. Instead, resentment began to take root. Leaning on Christ was a day-by-day challenge he was still working to get right. And with the way things were spiraling out of control it was getting harder by the minute.

A knock on the door jerked Ty from his brooding. "Come in."

Nick entered the room carrying a tray of food. "Chloe thought you might be hungry."

Ty glanced at the covered dish and glass of milk and felt his stomach churn. "Not really, though I do appreciate the offer."

Nick handed him the tray despite his disinclination. "Take my advice and eat what you can. Facing what seems to be an uphill battle might take away your appetite, but you can't afford to get sick."

Ty offered him a wry grin. "Did Chloe tell you to say that as well?"

Nick laughed. "Apparently you know my wife."

"Enough to know I'll never be able to repay her. . .or you." Ty set the tray in his lap and felt a twinge of appetite return as he took off the cover and the savory aroma filled his senses. Meatloaf and mashed potatoes would go a long way to keep up his stamina. "Both of you have gone far beyond the role of lawyer and hostess."

"Don't worry about it." Nick leaned against the doorframe. "I would have done the same for someone else. Well, I might not share my wife's meatloaf with just anyone, but hey. . .what are friends for?"

Ty took a bite and smiled. "I can see why you're not keen on sharing your wife's cooking."

"And we've got some cherry cobbler as well if you'd like to join us in the living room."

"I just might do that." Ty took a second bite then held up his fork. "Can I ask you a spiritual question first?"

"You bet." Nick slid into the rocking chair, pushing the footstool aside with his heel.

"I'm sure Chloe told you Christianity is a new thing for me." Ty stabbed at a green bean, then frowned. "I guess the bottom line is that I'm grappling here as to how to justify God's presence in my life when I'm in the midst of losing everything I have."

Nick blew out a long breath. "I'd say that's a question man's tried to work out for centuries. Where's God in the midst of pain?"

Ty nodded, certain there wasn't going to be a simple answer to his problem. "I feel as if God has abandoned me and expects me to figure things out on my own."

Nick leaned forward to rest his elbows on his knees. "I don't think I've ever told anyone this, but before Brandon was born, Chloe had a miscarriage. It was one of the worst experiences of my life. Realizing I'd never be able to hold the child we'd waited and prayed for was hard. Watching Chloe suffer was even worse. She went through a time of severe depression, and I was helpless to do anything about it. I asked myself some of the very same questions you have to be asking yourself right now."

"So what did you do?"

"I was forced to answer one challenging question. Did I believe God was in control of everything, including His plans for my family? The truth was, if God wasn't in control of everything, I had no reason to continue to follow Him. In the end it boiled down to a simple matter of faith."

"We live by faith and not by sight." Ty poked at the mashed potatoes with his fork, finding the words hard to come to terms with. "That's a tough concept to grasp. Especially for someone used to dealing with concrete numbers and facts."

"Or like a lawyer forced to deal only in evidence?" Nick leaned back in the chair and shook his head. "We want something we can hold on to, but God's ways are never man's. I made myself look back at other times in my life when God's presence was unmistakable. He didn't leave me then, and every day I choose to believe He won't leave me now, either. Listen—I know you're not looking for a sermon here, but Hebrews says we're to hold unswervingly to the hope we profess, for He who promised is faithful. Nothing you experience here on earth can begin to compare with the reward of heaven Christ has in store for us."

Ty set the tray on the bed beside him and tried to digest

everything Nick said. "I can't say my faith has been holding steady these past few days."

"The Bible also says we are blessed when we persevere under trial, because we will receive the crown of life God has promised to those who love Him. It's worth it, Ty."

"Deep down I know it's worth it." Ty looked up and caught Nick's gaze. "But what if the court convicts me? I'll have lost my job, my reputation, and Kayla. . . ."

He squeezed his eyes shut at the reminder. Losing Kayla would always be what hurt the most.

"I don't know, Ty. All I can do is promise to do everything in my power to ensure the truth becomes known." Nick rocked back in the chair. "Have you thought about calling Kayla? She has to be frantic."

"The message she left on my answering machine made it quite clear as to what role she wants me to play in her life." As much as he didn't want to admit it, things were over between the two of them, and he respected her enough to step out of her life if that's what she wanted.

Nick cocked his head. "What's the old saying? It's a woman's prerogative to change her mind? I wouldn't give up on her yet."

"More wisdom from Chloe?"

Nick's boisterous chuckle filled the room. "If it were up to her, she'd plunk the two of you down in a locked room together and keep you in there until you work it out. She hates seeing her friend hurt. And besides that, I'd say she's developed a bit of a soft spot for you for some reason."

Ty let out a deep sigh, wishing he could say the same for Kayla after all that had transpired in the past twenty-four hours. "It's nice to know a couple of people are in my corner."

"We'll get you through this." Nick stood and clasped Ty's

shoulder. "Keep your eyes fixed on Him. He'll never leave you."

"I'll keep reminding myself."

"And for the record." Nick stopped in the doorway. "I think Chloe's right about Kayla. Sometimes you have to take a chance. It's not as if you're going to lose anything."

"You've got a point there." Ty grabbed his cell phone out of his back pocket and stared at the number pad. "Maybe it is time I took that chance."

&

By the fourth phone call, Ty felt the lump of concern in his chest begin to swell. Where was Kayla? He'd called her cell phone, but no one had answered. Next he tried her mom's house, her office phone, and even Jenny.

He stalked down the narrow hallway and into the living room where Nick was working through some files at his desk. "Something's happened to Kayla."

Chloe jumped up from the floor where she'd been reading a book to her boys and moved beside her husband. "What are you talking about?"

"I don't know for sure." Ty rubbed the back of his neck wondering when the nightmare of the past twenty-four hours would disappear. "I can't get a hold of her, and no one has seen her."

Nick took off his reading glasses and swiveled the chair away from the desk. "She's probably running errands for tonight's event. She mentioned it yesterday." He looked to his wife. "What was it?"

"They're catering the Walker/James wedding."

Ty leaned against the half wall that separated the living room from the entryway. If something had happened to her because of his involvement with Abbott, he'd never forgive himself. What if subtle warnings had just escalated into a calculated attempt to silence Ty?

Beads of sweat collected on his forehead. "What if Abbott got to her?"

Nick shook his head. "There's no reason for Abbott to call attention to himself at this point. If he's guilty he's got you where he wants you. His best move is to stay out of things, and he's smart enough to know that."

Ty wasn't convinced. "I spoke with Jenny a minute ago. She's at the church, and she hasn't seen Kayla for the past four hours. You know Kayla. She'd never leave a job without telling someone where she's going. Even Jenny's getting frantic."

"Where was the last place Jenny saw her?"

Ty worked to steady his breathing. "Jenny said they spoke after lunch at the church, and Kayla told Jenny she needed an hour or so by herself to pray. Jenny went back to finish up some of the food for tonight, but when she returned with the rest of the staff Kayla wasn't around and she hadn't finished any of the wedding stuff. All she could figure was that she went to the church's prayer room and fell asleep. We all know how tired she's been lately. She went to check on her but saw no sign of her. That was twenty minutes ago."

Chloe dug into the pocket of her jeans then tossed her husband the car keys. "I'll stay with the boys and make some phone calls. You two go find Kayla."

Ten minutes later Ty and Nick pulled into the church parking lot. With the wedding scheduled to start within the next two hours the parking lot was already filling up with some of the wedding party.

Jenny was inside pacing the kitchen floor, her cell phone pressed against her ear. She held up her finger and motioned for them to wait. A moment later she snapped the phone shut. "She's never done this before. I've called everyone I can think of; no one's seen her, and she isn't in the building."

"What about her car?"

"It's gone as well. None of this makes sense. We all know she was under a lot of pressure lately, but she'd never walk out on a job. Never."

Ty still hadn't shelved his theory that Abbott was involved. "Show me where you think she was last."

Jenny stumbled from the kitchen, then scurried down the center aisle of the church auditorium. In the dim light of the room a half dozen people bustled around, making final touches in preparation for the ceremony. The door to the prayer room was half open. Jenny pushed it the rest of the way, then slipped in before them.

"As I told Ty I can't be certain this is where she went, but she headed this way, and it's a place she likes to come when she needs a few moments of peace."

Ty glanced around the room. Approximately six by six, the room was painted in subtle hues of blue, with no furnishings other than a wooden bench and three other chairs. A large painting of the cross hung on the back wall. On either side, light filtered through to stained-glass windowpanes. The only other thing in the room was a potted plant in the corner. No place to hide anything. No clues that even placed her in the room.

He glanced behind the ceramic pot just in case. "Wait a minute."

"What is it?" Jenny stepped up beside him.

Ty bent down and picked up a cell phone that had fallen behind the plant. He didn't have to take a second look to know it was Kayla's. "She's been here."

The phone had a long crack along the side. Something

had happened in this room. Ty's own cell phone rang, and he reached into his pocket to answer it.

"Ty, this is Penny. Abbott's got Kayla."

fifteen

Ty parked his car at the marina, then checked the time on the dashboard. He had three minutes to spare. Penny's instructions had been explicit. Twenty minutes to get there. Find his friend's boat, the *Angelina*. And come alone. Any signs of police involvement meant he'd never see Kayla alive again. He felt for the tiny tape recorder in his front pocket that Nick had handed him at the church and wondered if he'd made the right decision to bring it. Abbott wasn't a fool, and Ty wasn't willing to risk Kayla's life. Even if it meant Abbott won in the end.

He moved to the end of the floating walkway, replaying Penny's message over and over in his head. The thought that Penny might be involved sent a shudder of fear through him. He was still uncertain if his former secretary was simply being used as a pawn in Richard Abbott's game or if she'd been on his side all along.

Either way Kayla's life was in danger.

He stared out across the blue waters of the harbor, took in the details of the scene and remembered all the summer days he'd spent out on the ocean with his parents. Somewhere, among the dozens of boats, was Kayla. It took him two and a half minutes to locate the *Angelina*. The sleek vessel was tied up at the end of one of the floating walkways, not in its usual slip. Convenient if Abbott was planning a quick getaway. But how did he find the key?

Abbott sat near the helm wearing a sweater and khaki

pants. If it were possible, the man looked worse than the day Ty had walked out of the office on him. Pallid skin, thick jowls, thinning hair, all signs of stress. . .and guilt as far as he was concerned. Penny stood beside him, her hand possessively on his arm.

Where was the loyal secretary he'd worked with for three years? He'd considered her a friend. "You've been in on this all along, Penny?"

Penny avoided Ty's gaze. "What can I say? Abbott pays well."

"Glad you could make it, Ty. Your friend's boat is a beauty." Abbott pulled off his sunglasses. "I'm considering making an offer on one myself. Of course, I'm prepared to put out quite a bit more on a bigger one. Oh, and if you're wondering how I got the key, well, let's just say I have my ways." He laughed.

Ty drew in a deep breath. *Where are You, God?*

He stepped onto the familiar boat wishing the marina weren't so quiet. The weather was too cold for most people to consider going out today despite a clear sky and calm sea. Somehow Abbott had even managed to use the weather to his advantage.

Abbott tapped a gun at his side. "Don't get too close, please, Ty. I wouldn't want anything to happen to you."

"Where's Kayla?" He refused to play the old man's games.

"Twenty-eight feet, pedestal steering, three-blade propeller—"

"I said, where's Kayla?"

"You always were so focused on the task at hand, weren't you, Ty? You need to relax. That's what I've done. Look at me. I've shed the tie and suit jacket and replaced it with something a bit more casual. Why? Because I realized life's too short to follow the rules."

"You know I couldn't care less about your plans to spend

more of the company's money, Abbott. I want—"

"I know. You want Kayla." He finished the last sip from a wine glass as he maneuvered the boat away from the dock and toward the open waters. "Search him first, Penny."

Ty stood rigid as Penny patted him down. She drew the tape recorder from his jacket pocket and threw it onto the deck.

"I'm disappointed, Ty." Abbott twisted the stem of his wine glass between his fingers and shook his head as Penny stepped away from Ty. "Weren't my instructions explicit enough? Twenty minutes. Come alone. No police. Did you actually think a tape recorder fit into the equation? I'm tempted to end this whole thing right now without your ever seeing Kayla."

Ty pressed his lips together, certain that any signs of begging on his part would only end up provoking the man.

Abbott waved his hand in Penny's direction. "Bring her out, Penny. Though I will warn you, Ty. Don't try anything else foolish. Trust me. You'll regret it."

Thirty seconds later Kayla stumbled onto the deck in front of Penny. Ty moved to help her, but Abbott reached out and stopped him with the barrel of his gun.

The boat rocked beneath him. Ty forced himself to stay where he was, his focus now on Kayla. "Are you all right?"

Kayla nodded, then took a seat where Penny told her. When had life spun so completely out of control that he'd been the cause of Kayla's kidnapping? He could see the fear in her eyes, mixed with hope that he'd do something to save them both. His head began to pound. Nothing made sense. Kayla sitting with her arms tied behind her; Penny taking orders from Richard Abbott.

Abbott, on the other hand, seemed to feel no remorse

over the situation. "Penny's the perfect secretary, you know, especially when it comes to gathering information from the enemy."

Ty decided to ignore the implications. All he knew was that he'd trusted Penny, and she'd betrayed him.

Just as he'd betrayed Kayla.

Ty tried unsuccessfully to swallow the lump in his throat. A little of his own medicine perhaps? He hated the fact that he'd hurt her. Hated more that he was the cause of her being hurt again. If only he'd been able to protect her. . . . "So what happens now?

Abbott slid his sunglasses back on as the shoreline grew smaller. "I suppose you have the right to know. I'm just sorry I don't have the time to let the law take care of things. It would have been nice to see you rot in jail the next twenty years. That's what you'd planned for me, isn't it?"

Ty shook his head. "I have the right to know what?"

"Face it, Ty. With all the bad publicity the company is looking at right now because of your case, shareholders are nervous. I can't let the company go bankrupt. I have to think of its future."

"You should have been thinking about the future of the company when you stole from its assets." Ty took a step toward Kayla. "Besides, you can't seriously think you'll get away with this."

"Trust Me."

Ty felt a tiny seed of confidence grow. This wasn't over yet. What had Nick said? It all boiled down to a simple matter of faith. Either God was in control of everything, or faith in Him was empty. He was going to choose to walk by faith.

He took another step forward.

"Stay where you are." Abbott held up his gun and shook

his head. "Here's how I see it. I've already managed to create enough evidence to keep the DA, the SEC, and whatever other organization you can think of busy with evidence to convict you. They'll find some of the money—enough to satisfy them—in an offshore account connected to you. So, yes, I know I'll get away with it. The whole world now knows that Ty Lawrence is nothing more than another power-hungry executive who tried to make a fortune the wrong way. You'll never be able to stand up to the big boys."

"Think what you like, but you know you can't get away with this."

"Oh, really?" Abbott cut the engine, walked across the deck and shoved Kayla's chin up with the butt of his handgun. "Because here's the way it's going to play out, and, frankly, you don't have any way to stop me."

He pulled a folded piece of paper from his pocket with a gloved hand. "This is a signed confession and suicide note, written by none other than Ty Lawrence. No one will question when a man recently arrested and facing the reality of spending the next few decades in jail kills himself on his friend's boat after murdering his ex-fiancée. Penny was always so good at passing along information, like the fact that your friend's boat, the *Angelina,* is docked here for the winter."

"Why this boat?"

"It's the perfect place for a murder/suicide, isn't it? And saves me a cleaning bill for the mess you'll leave behind. With that and the physical evidence the police will have no problems proving the theory correct." Abbott leaned against the railing, looking confident. "Once I am cleared of being involved in any wrongdoing, I'll be free to leave the country. Health reasons, you know. The doctor says I'm working too hard. I'll resign from my position as CEO; then I can spend my millions where no one can touch me."

A cold wave of horror swept over Ty, but he wasn't willing to end things yet. "The police won't stop looking for all the money, and eventually you'll slip. One day they'll tie it to you."

Abbott moved back toward the helm. "Maybe, but $175 million is worth the risk, don't you think? Though if you hadn't started turning in data to the police, I'd planned to wait around until I had at least a quarter of a billion."

Ty glanced at Kayla. He couldn't stand seeing her sit there with her hands tied behind her back and a bruise marking her cheek. All he had left to fight with were his words. "I don't think any amount of money is worth the risk. And there's something else I find interesting. You taught me everything I know about negotiating. Surely you don't think I'll simply agree to go along with your little plan."

"Penny, tie him up. I don't want you to finish your grim deed, Ty, until we're out to sea." Abbott glanced at his watch. "Don't worry, though. It will all be over in thirty minutes. We've got another boat coming to pick us up, but of course you won't need a ride at that point, will you?"

Ty felt a shudder whiz like a bullet up his spine. The man was insane.

Penny grabbed a length of rope and had Ty sit in a chair beside Kayla. "You know you can still get out of this, Penny."

Penny looked at him. "Last time I heard, the law doesn't take too kindly to premeditated murder. I'd say that puts me in pretty deep."

Abbott laughed as Penny wrapped the rope around Ty's wrists. "You could have had all of this, Ty. Never understood that storing-up-treasures-in-heaven garbage. Seems to me this is reality and enjoying it right now makes a lot more sense."

"Except heaven's real, too, Abbott. Just like hell."

Ignoring Ty's response, Abbott called to Penny to throw him another drink from the cooler. She grabbed one and tossed it toward Abbott, but her aim was too long. Distracted, Abbott turned to catch the bottle. Ty scrambled to untie the rope before Penny could tighten the knot. There was no time to think. He lunged for Abbott. Caught off guard, the portly man didn't have a chance. Ty slammed into his right side. Abbott's attempted shot clipped the bow of the boat.

Ty kicked the gun out of the man's hand and shoved him to the ground face down. Within seconds two federal agents appeared on deck from the cabin below. One of them jerked Abbott to his feet then slapped a pair of handcuffs onto his wrists. The man was still trying to catch his breath as the other agent radioed for backup then read him his rights.

Ty hurried to release Kayla. "Are you all right?" He drew her into his arms, needing to convince himself she was alive and this was over.

"I think so." She slid her wrists out of the first knot. "What is going on?"

"I have no idea, but with Abbott in handcuffs something must be going right finally."

As soon as the rope came off, Kayla reached up and wrapped her arms around Ty's neck. "I've never been so glad to see you in my entire life."

He looked down at her and tilted up her chin with his thumb. "Does that mean you forgive me?"

Her smile worked to melt the anger that bubbled inside him toward Abbott. All that mattered anymore was that she was okay.

She nodded her head. "I let fear blind me from the truth. Deep down I knew you were innocent. I just hate that it took a crazy man to show me the truth."

He pulled her close, relishing in the softness of her hair, the sweetness of her perfume, and the touch of her skin. "It wasn't your fault, Kayla. I should have told you the entire truth a long time ago."

"Yes, you should have."

He ran his finger down her cheek. "I promise I won't keep things from you ever again. In wanting to protect you and our relationship I almost lost you. It's a matter of trust, something I want our marriage to be based on."

"Is that a proposal?"

"I'm sorry to interrupt, Ty." Penny walked toward them, the bottom of her windbreaker flapping in the wind. "You did well. I'm sorry you both had to go through what you did, but we got him. The entire conversation was being recorded. Richard Abbott isn't going to see the outside of a prison for a very long time."

He shook his head, his arm tightening around Kayla's waist. "That's wonderful, but I don't understand, Penny. You're working for the government?"

"Retired Petty Officer Penelope Waterford at your service, sir." She saluted as one of the uniformed agents approached. "And I'm sorry about the phone calls and the encounter at the restaurant."

Kayla's eyes widened. "That was you?"

"Pretty good disguise, wasn't it?" She shook her head as one of the agents dragged Abbott off the boat. "Abbott thought he needed to send warnings that showed he could get to you whenever he wanted to. In order to ensure he continued to trust me I had to go along with it."

"Penny was honorably discharged from the navy three years ago." The stocky blond man shook Ty's and Kayla's hands, introducing himself as Agent Stevenson with the Securities and Exchange Commission. "We recruited her to help take down Abbott from the inside. Unfortunately, he's good, and we always seemed to be a step behind him. When Abbott told Penny what he planned to do, she came up with this plan and hid us down below. She vouched for your innocence the whole time. I'm glad to see she was right."

Ty felt himself relax as the boat sped back to the marina. The reality of spending the next twenty years in jail began to fade. "What about the charges against me?"

The man repositioned the bill of his baseball cap. "I'll need you both to give a complete statement, but I don't think it will take much to convince the DA and the government that you're innocent, Mr. Lawrence. And Abbott won't be going anywhere for a long time."

The second officer docked the boat, then shut off the motor. "I need to ask the two of you to move off the boat. We'll let you know when our men are finished, but for now it's a crime scene."

છે

Kayla ignored the throb in her head as Ty helped her off the boat and focused instead on how everything in her life had just changed—again—in the past ten minutes. A test of faith? Perseverance in the midst of adversity? Whatever it had been, she felt as if she'd failed the exam.

"I'm sorry, Ty."

He wrapped his arm around her shoulder. "For what?"

She looked up at him, afraid he'd disappear and she'd wake up in the boat again. "For not believing you."

"I'm the one who should be asking for your forgiveness. I should have told you the government had questioned me. I just never imagined things getting this out of control."

She laced her fingers in his as they slowly walked down the floating walkway toward the other end of the marina. "I'm still reeling from everything. I thought you were guilty, and then Penny was involved."

He leaned down and kissed the top of her head. "I'm sorry about all of this."

"As long as we're all okay." She breathed in the salty sea air that mingled with his aftershave lotion.

"So." Ty stepped off the walkway and turned her toward him. "Where were we when Penny, my former secretary-turned-criminal-accomplice-turned-hero so rudely interrupted us?"

The gentle waves lapped against the shore. A seagull cried out overhead. But all she saw at the moment was Ty. "If I remember correctly I think you were proposing."

"Was I?"

"Yes, you were. And I was about to say yes." She shot him a wide smile.

"Well, if you were about to say yes, then I'd better hurry up and pop the question."

Kayla looked up at him. Her toes tingled with anticipation, and her heart felt as if it were about to fly out of her chest.

"Kayla Rose Marceilo, the worst thing that's happened to me in the past forty-eight hours was the thought of losing you. It seemed worse than the pending trial or even facing the reality I might go to jail. I need you to be a part of my life, because I love you." He brushed back a strand of hair the wind had blown across her cheek. "You help me be a better man, Kayla, and I want to spend the rest of my life with you."

Kayla felt her chest swell with emotion as she gazed into his eyes. "Ty, there's nothing else I'd rather do than spend the rest of my life with you."

Ty pulled her into his arms and gently kissed her on the lips. "I take it that's a yes?"

"Oh yes, Ty." She giggled as he kissed her again. "Definitely a yes."

sixteen

Kayla stood in front of the full-length mirror and fingered one of the small pearls that graced the sleeves. The satin skirt, with its trail of roses and silver leaves, served as a reminder that God really had worked things together for good. In the past three months Ty had been exonerated by the government, and her mother, while still not back to work, was able to walk again.

Kayla felt a ripple of peace flow through her. Nightmares from the day Richard Abbott had grabbed her from the prayer room had completely vanished. No longer was her heart overcome with fear of the future. Instead she saw only possibilities and the rich future she and Ty could have together.

Jenny walked into the sunlit dressing room carrying the veil.

"It's breathtaking, isn't it?" Kayla gathered the skirt and spun around to face her friend. Today she really did feel like a princess about to marry her prince. No more doubts or uncertainties. Only a calm assurance she was following God's will.

"So how does it feel to know that in less than an hour you'll be Mrs. Ty Lawrence?" Jenny asked.

Kayla's smile reached the corners of her eyes. "Like I'm flying on top of the world."

"I'm glad to hear that." Jenny handed Kayla the same gauzy veil with rhinestones and drop pearls she'd first admired at the boutique then helped her slip it on. "Though I'm still not sure how you were able to schedule your wedding before mine."

Kayla laughed. "Because I've always wanted a Valentine's Day wedding, and I'm not waiting another twelve months."

Jenny nudged Kayla with her elbow. "I should have agreed with your offer to have a double wedding."

Kayla smiled, then glanced at the clock on the wall. The forty-five minutes left until the ceremony seemed like forever. Lifting up the front of her dress so she wouldn't trip, she headed for the small balcony outside the room.

Jenny hurried behind her with Kayla's satin slippers. "Where are you going?"

"I just want to take a peek and make sure everything is ready." Giddy excitement wouldn't allow her to stay cooped up in the small room any longer.

"Chloe is down there right now, double-checking everything, and besides Ty is going to see you if you stand there."

Ignoring her friend's counsel, Kayla leaned against the railing and glanced over the balcony onto the wooden church pews where Jenny and Chloe had transformed the simple sanctuary with roses, white organza, and candles. Soon the lights would dim, and the string quartet would start playing. It was everything she'd ever imagined her wedding day to be.

"Kayla?"

She ducked behind the railing at the sound of Ty's voice. "Ty? You're not supposed to see me yet."

"What?"

Jenny leaned over the balcony. "She said you're not supposed to see her yet. It's bad luck for the groom to see the bride before the ceremony."

"Tell her I don't believe in bad luck."

Kayla crouched behind the wooden balcony rail, working to keep her balance without ripping her dress. "I don't either, but it's. . .tradition."

"What?"

Jenny pulled her cell phone from her pocket, punched in a number, then waited for it to ring.

Kayla glanced up at Jenny. "Who are you calling?"

A cell phone rang from below the balcony. "Ty, here's Kayla"

Kayla stared at the phone Jenny shoved in her hand. "Okay, isn't this a bit silly?"

Ty laughed on the other end of the line. "I agree. Tell your friend she's nuts."

Kayla pressed the phone to her ear. "I could give her the phone, and you could tell her—"

"No!" Ty laughed. "I might not have you exactly where I want you, but at least I can hear your voice."

"Forty-five minutes and I'm yours."

"There's still the ceremony, the reception—"

"And a week in the Bahamas." Kayla moved back from the edge of the balcony and sat down in a chair, letting the yards of fabric swirl around her.

"Now you're talking." The line was quiet for a moment. "Kayla?"

"Yes?"

"I love you."

"I love you, too."

Kayla clicked the phone shut and sent a prayer of thanks to God that everything was right in the world.

A Letter To Our Readers

Dear Reader:

In order that we might better contribute to your reading enjoyment, we would appreciate your taking a few minutes to respond to the following questions. We welcome your comments and read each form and letter we receive. When completed, please return to the following:

Fiction Editor
Heartsong Presents
PO Box 719
Uhrichsville, Ohio 44683

1. Did you enjoy reading *A Matter of Trust* by Lisa Harris?
   ❏ Very much! I would like to see more books by this author!
   ❏ Moderately. I would have enjoyed it more if

   _____

   _____

   _____

2. Are you a member of **Heartsong Presents**?   ❏ Yes   ❏ No
   If no, where did you purchase this book? _____

   _____

3. How would you rate, on a scale from 1 (poor) to 5 (superior), the cover design? _____

4. On a scale from 1 (poor) to 10 (superior), please rate the following elements.

   ____ Heroine   ____ Plot
   ____ Hero   ____ Inspirational theme
   ____ Setting   ____ Secondary characters

5. These characters were special because? _____
_____
_____

6. How has this book inspired your life? _____
_____
_____

7. What settings would you like to see covered in future
   Heartsong Presents books? _____
_____
_____

8. What are some inspirational themes you would like to see
   treated in future books? _____
_____
_____

9. Would you be interested in reading other **Heartsong
   Presents** titles? ❑ Yes   ❑ No

10. Please check your age range:
    ❑ Under 18   ❑ 18-24
    ❑ 25-34   ❑ 35-45
    ❑ 46-55   ❑ Over 55

Name _____
Occupation _____
Address _____
City, State, Zip_____

KANSAS WEDDINGS

3 stories in 1

Three Kansas women have difficult decisions to make and burdens to bear. Will these women find love despite their handships?

Contemporary, paperback, 352 pages, 5³/₁₆" x 8"

Heart♥ong

HEARTSONG PRESENTS TITLES AVAILABLE NOW:

Presents

HEARTSONG
PRESENTS

If you love Christian romance…

$10.⁹⁹

You'll love Heartsong Presents' inspiring and faith-filled romances by today's very best Christian authors. . .Wanda E. Brunstetter, Mary Connealy, Susan Page Davis, Cathy Marie Hake, and Joyce Livingston, to mention a few!

When you join Heartsong Presents, you'll enjoy four brand-new, mass market, 176-page books—two contemporary and two historical—that will build you up in your faith when you discover God's role in every relationship you read about!

Imagine. . .four new romances every four weeks—with men and women like you who long to meet the one God has chosen as the love of their lives…all for the low price of $10.99 postpaid.

Mass Market 176 Pages

To join, simply visit www.heartsong presents.com or complete the coupon below and mail it to the address provided.

✂ -

YES! Sign me up for Heart♥ng!

NEW MEMBERSHIPS WILL BE SHIPPED IMMEDIATELY!
Send no money now. We'll bill you only $10.99 postpaid with your first shipment of four books. Or for faster action, call 1-740-922-7280.

NAME_____

ADDRESS_____

CITY_____STATE_____ZIP_____

MAIL TO: HEARTSONG PRESENTS, P.O. Box 721, Uhrichsville, Ohio 44683
or sign up at **WWW.HEARTSONGPRESENTS.COM**